Where Am I?

By

Sue Lacey

To Sue,
Best wishes,
Sue Lacey.

Acknowledgements and grateful thanks to my family for their technical assistance and encouragement.

Though many of the places are real, the characters and events in this book are purely fictitious.

Chapter One.

Where am I?
       Why am I here?
          Who am I?
All I can feel is my body, shaking with cold, shaking with the fear of not knowing the answer to any of these questions.

When I look around me all I can see is blackness… is this night time, or am I just in a dark place? Whichever it is I feel uncomfortable, I feel scared. Whatever has brought me to this place I know it feels wrong, and that I really don't want to be here?

I feel another deep shiver of fear running down my body, adding to the cold and the agony of not knowing where and why I am here in this terrible, scary place, or how to escape from it.

But then I realise that there is still one thing even more terrifying; I have no idea, none at all, of who I am!

The fear of this is worse than any other and I can feel it spreading through my mind like a mist descending across a bare, empty space.

The one comfort to be gained from so much fear is that at least it means I'm alive, but who am I?

Why don't I remember this?

All I can do is lie still and calm my mind and try to let it settle, then perhaps I can come up with some answers to all this.

Suddenly I can hear noises, perhaps footsteps though I can't be sure of that, coming towards me. Should I call out, or perhaps I should keep quiet? Not knowing my situation makes me unsure which course of action to take.

It could be the footsteps of someone I know coming to help me. On the other hand, if these are footsteps, I am aware of the possibility of them belonging to someone who means me harm.

I wait, listening in the hope of hearing something to give me a clue as to what the noises were and who or what has made them.

As suddenly as they came they seemed to be going away again. Maybe it's worth the risk. Hesitantly, but hopefully, I call out,

"Hello, can anybody hear me?"

No response. The footsteps are still moving away.

"Please, somebody, please help me, don't go away."

If there was anyone there I get no response. Either they can't hear me, or for whatever reason, choose to ignore my pleas for help. Perhaps they weren't footsteps at all.

And now everything is silent, deathly silent, not a sound to be heard.

Once again I'm left in this satanical darkness, alone and unknowing of all that I am or all that I should be. I have to concentrate, work this out, try to be calm and logical. Bearing in mind that I don't even know if I am a calm and logical person this could prove difficult!

Ideally my first priority is to try to remember who I am.

No, it's no use: try as I might my mind is a complete blank, and it is all I can do to stop myself going into a complete meltdown in the attempt.

I must have an identity, everyone has an identity, but it's as if I've been wiped of this in the same way as a hacker can wipe everything from the memory of a computer.

Have I got anything on me, perhaps in a pocket? What about labels on clothes etc.? No, I can feel that the pockets on what I believe are a pair of denim jeans are empty. As for labels or any other distinguishable clues, I can feel none, and anyway it is far too dark to see any of these things exist.

Ok, at least I can try to find out what my surroundings are. Until now I have not dared to move. For whatever reason I have been lying down since I first came round. Maybe I had been in a coma or under anaesthetic. That could account for my loss of memory but, if so, why was everything so dark now that I'm conscious? Perhaps I've gone blind, or perhaps I'm actually dead and passing into another life! That would at least explain why no one heard my calls.

Now I know my mind is unhinged! Do I really believe in a life after death? How do I know whether I do or not when I don't know who I am?

Tentatively, without moving my body, I reach out and feel around me. I can feel nothing within reach to my sides or above me which is any different to the surface under me. I feel what I am lying on and find the surface is cold, hard and damp, probably some sort of stone or rock. As I cannot feel any sides to this that could put me in danger of falling off, I reckon it's safe to sit up, but before I reach an upright position I am startled by a sudden loud, almost thunderous, noise making me jump up and causing my head to come into sharp contact with something above me, equally as hard as the surface I am on. All I can do now is to crouch, huddled up, dazed and confused, desperately trying to keep myself from losing consciousness again.

As I feel my head I can feel a warm trickle of blood finding its way toward my left eye, but when I feel across toward my right eye there is no warm trickle but just a cold sticky feel, perhaps indicating an earlier crack on the head. Maybe that would explain my loss of memory. Yet none of this explains where I am or how I came to be in such an awful situation.

Staying in a crouched position I crawl carefully around, feeling for clues, feeling for a way out of here. After all, I figure that if I got here it stands to reason I must be able to get out. If it was something I'd fallen into, an old mine shaft for instance, then I wouldn't feel the rocks across the

4

top of me. I reason that there must be another way out of here somewhere, so proceed to crawl about on my hands and knees feeling for this.

Whatever this place is it has to be pretty big but, just as I am at the point of admitting defeat, the wall appears to come to a sudden end, turning at right angles to the one I'm following. I reach across to my left and just within arm's reach can feel another going parallel to this.

Ah, at last. Is this some sort of passage way… perhaps the way I'd come in to here in the first place? Realising that this is possibly the only way out I know I must follow it, though as I do so, on all fours, I find the surface to be a mass of loose rough bits of rock which cut into the skin of my hands and knees. There is also a strange odour in the air, what air there is. No time to stay here wondering about strange odours, I need to get out of here, wherever here is, and anyway the sharp surface I'm on is overtaking my other senses.

This pain continues for what must be quite a few metres, as does the head space, but soon comes to an end, or so it feels. Suddenly the passageway feels blocked by piles of loose rock. Now I think I'm aware of the cause of the odour I'd smelled…I believe dynamite has been used in here, but did whoever did this know I was in here; surely not.

I've got to get out of here, I don't know how but I must try. I spend what seems an age digging away the sharp, smashed up stone from the passageway, tearing my hands in the process, but driven on by desperation and the will to

5

survive. Suddenly there's a mini rock slide causing me to pull back for a second or two before creeping forward on my knees to investigate the results. A feeling of relief sweeps over me as I can feel there is just a small gap at the top of the pile of debris, a gap through which I think I can actually feel the first taste of something nearer fresh air, but is this gap anywhere near big enough for me to wriggle through? Frantically I dig again with my poor, sore hands, going at my task like a terrier digging out rabbits, and eventually heave an exhausted sigh of relief as I feel there is now just room enough for me to squeeze through.

Unfortunately I still find myself in darkness, and still on my sore hands and knees, but I know I have no choice but to hang on to the hope that I'm heading in the right direction to free myself.

I dare to reach up and find I can no longer touch the rock above me from my painful kneeling position. Tentatively I raise myself up using the rock wall to the side to support myself, and feel a surge of relief at getting my knees off of the broken-glass like surface I'd felt would never end. At least now I can add to my self-knowledge by the realisation that I am actually wearing a fairly substantial pair of trainers. Strangely enough I hadn't given much thought to my footwear but, after the extremely painful time spent on my poor hands and knees, the relief is ameliorating.

As I stand here, still in the pitch black, but glad to be upright at last, I begin to realise that I seem to be in a tunnel or cave, perhaps even a mine. Whatever it is, at least now I can stand up and walk, albeit with extreme caution, using my hands to guide me as my eyes certainly can't.

My throat is so dry, parched is an understatement, but all I can do is run my hands down the damp rocks surrounding me, then hold them to my mouth to moisten my lips. I've no idea when I last drank anything. All I can do is to keep going on the way I'm going as there seems no other way. Perhaps if I ever find a way out, find daylight, I might be more aware of what has brought me here in the first place and, more importantly, just who I am.

Allowing my concentration to drift proves a big mistake. Whack… my head comes into hard contact again with a particularly low and sharp rock above. I forgot to feel with my hands and left it to my poor head again instead. Ouch! I wish I'd not done that, especially as I can feel the warm trickle of blood down my forehead again. Until now I believe that which I'd felt earlier had stopped. Even so, this is the same place I knocked just now, not the one which I must have had much earlier, the one that had caused the great sore lump on the side of my head that I'd found earlier.

As I creep slowly onwards, hoping this is the right direction, I begin to despair of my own survival. I pray I am not going away from the exit that my brain reasons there must be. Suddenly the way I'm following seems to take a downward tilt, a thing I find unnerving. Perhaps I need to go back the way I came but to my relief, just as I reach what seems to be the lowest point, my luck takes a much needed change for the better.

My foot feels suddenly quite wet. I step back one step and crouch down to find the cause of this and am relieved to feel my hand in water. At this low point it seems the dampness of the walls has collected in a pool at the bottom. What a lifesaver! Cupping my hands together I reach down and scoop up a much needed drink. Pleased to find it tasted quite fresh, I lower myself to the ground and reach forward to enable me to use both hands, desperate to quench my lip-cracking thirst.

I stay like this until, having drunk my fill, I sit back against the rock taking a rest. Before moving off again I take the opportunity to freshen myself up as best I can, paying particular attention to my blood soaked face. All I can hope is that this will make me look reasonably acceptable if I ever escape my nightmare.

After a while, though I realise I should move on, I feel reluctant to do so and can feel a deep sense of exhaustion sweeping over me and, though I have no desire to prolong my ordeal, find I have the need to sit back against the rock wall behind me. I just have no strength to fight it any more and soon find myself sinking back into a deep sleep.

Just how long this lasted I have no idea, but as I come to, hoping to find this has all been a terrible dream, I find nothing has changed. I'm still in the same dark, damp place, still with no answers to the questions I started with…where, why, who!

Chapter Two.

Taking one last drink I make up my mind to carry on whilst physically able to do so. After all, as I see it, I have three choices. I can go back the way I came, but the thought of that sends shivers down my spine. I can sit down here and stay where I am, but that would be giving in. No, I have to go on, wherever it takes me, this really is the only logical thing to do, possibly the only way to survive.

In a state of sheer exhaustion, pain and desperation, I force myself to put one foot in front of the other, taking care to feel for headspace as I go. Before going more than a matter of steps I find the path is leading me back upwards. Up to what I can't say, but this has got to be better than going down. I'm soon proved right in this assumption as, unless it's my imagination, I believe the way ahead is beginning to show just a slight glimmer of light in the distance. In anticipation of a final escape I manage to dig deep for the energy to keep going in this direction, and am soon rewarded with a positive sight of daylight coming through a good sized opening up ahead.

In what can only be a matter of a few minutes I emerge out of my rock prison into sunlight so bright that I have to close my eyes for a few seconds to let them become accustom to the light. When I manage to take a squinting look around me at my surroundings, I really was hoping to see something I recognised, something familiar, to tell me the answer to my first question of where am I ?

No, absolutely nothing rings any bells in my mind. There seems to be no sign of life at all visible. I'm surrounded by just rough and rocky landscape. My idea that where I had just come from was some sort of cave seems to be correct. Of course this still doesn't explain why I was in there, even less who I am!

At least though I can feel the warmth of the sunlight which is showing above a nearby hill and trickling through a copse of trees to my right. With a mixture of exhaustion and relief I drag myself across to a mossy mound, heave one almighty sigh, and collapse here, dropping into a deep, sound sleep.

I cannot say just how long I slept, but as I awoke I was aware of the warmth and the sound of a blackbird singing, and found myself praying that all of this would turn out to have been some sort of horrible nightmare. Just for that brief moment I convinced myself I would open my eyes and this time see familiar surroundings, maybe my own room, my own garden; just for that moment . . .

But that was not to be.

Almost reluctantly I opened my eyes again. At first the bright sunlight still blinded me after the darkness I had come from earlier. Where the sun had been creeping over the brow of the hill before, I must have slept for some time as it was now high in the sky above me.

When my eyes adjusted to the light I once again cast them all around me. Still I can see nothing I feel I know, nothing remotely familiar. If I knew in which direction to go perhaps I could find help and answers to my questions. All I can see, for as far as I can see is what looks like miles of hilly countryside covered in rocky outcrops. Not a sign of civilisation or signpost to point me in the direction of anywhere.

On rolling onto my knees to get to my feet I feel the burning pain from the time I'd spent crawling on them, which is also apparent by the torn appearance of my jeans. My hands are no better.

With no idea which way to go I reckon that, as I can see nothing much lower down the hill, perhaps the best plan would be to climb to the highest point in the hope of a better view of my surroundings from the other side of it. Picking my way slowly over the rough, rocky ground, I make my way upwards, feeling the heat on my back, until reaching the relief of the shelter from the small copse of trees covering the crown of the hill.

A few moments later I emerge on the far side of the trees and, as I had hoped, found myself looking down in the distance toward what looks like a fairly major road of some sort. If this is the case then I figure there must at some point be a reasonable sized town some way off in the distance well beyond my sight. All I can do is trudge off towards the base of the hill, and just keep walking in the hope of finding somewhere I know, or someone who could help me in some way. After all, perhaps this is where I came from, perhaps I actually live here somewhere and will find familiar sights, and perhaps people who will recognise me and bring my mind back in line, allow me to know who I am!

Wishing I'd had something to have collected some of that water in, I trudge off down the hill towards what I hope will be my salvation at last. At least the walking is much easier on this side of the hill. It's far more grass covered with very few of the rocky outcrops of the other side.

I feel as though I've been walking for miles, though as far as I know I could have been going in circles since coming down from the hills. Luckily, as I get further down I come to the road. I convince myself I can hear the very distant sounds of everyday life coming from a town but maybe this is wishful thinking as it is must still be some way ahead of me. I see vehicles coming, presumably travelling in and out of the town. Perhaps I can hitch a lift the last bit of the journey there?

It seems to have taken forever to reach the road on which these vehicles are hurtling along, by which time I'm feeling fit to drop. Finding a convenient tree by the roadside to offer some shade, I am relieved to sit with my back against it to rest before struggling on further. Feeling even more desperate for a drink but knowing there's none to be had, I must force myself on without it. Keeping in what little shade these few roadside trees offer, all I can do is to trudge on toward the town.

I must have walked some distance before my efforts to hitch a lift pay off when some sort of massive HGV pulled up alongside me. A rather scruffy looking middle aged driver eyed me up and down curiously before beckoning for me to climb aboard.

"Where you headed for girl'" he asked.

"I'm not really sure," I answer truthfully, "Just to the town up ahead I suppose, if you could drop me somewhere near please."

"I'm not going right to it, but I'll drop you off as near as I can," he says, and hardly before I get the door shut we're on our way.

I can't help feeling uncomfortable with the odd sideways glances he keeps giving me, to say nothing of the undeniable smirk that seems to cross his face when he does this. I suppose perhaps this is to be expected as I must look quite a sight, so I pretend I haven't noticed.

He didn't speak again, only to ask my name, a question I have no answer to, but instead of saying this I inexplicably find myself giving the first one that comes to mind, Jenny!

Where did that come from? Somehow I know Jenny is not really my name, but maybe I know the name from someone or somewhere. Anyway, it feels better to have a name rather than remain anonymous.

Before we come to a fork in the road my driver explains he needs to go right here, but I will need to follow the left fork towards town. He says he will pull into a layby round to the right for me to get out, and will show me the way I need to go from there. Being as we are on a dual carriageway this seems sensible and so I sit tight until he pulls into a layby on this much quieter road. To my surprise he jumps down from the cab and comes to my side to help me out . . . or so I think!

Once out he leads me into a small tree covered area where he says he will point me to the shortest route to the town.

"I reckon there's a few drops left in my flask might help you feel a bit better. I'll fetch that for us to share shall I?"

What a lifesaver, I'm thinking! It's not till he gets it out that I realise he means a hip flask with brandy in, not the water I really craved, and certainly not a flask of tea or coffee I was so desperate for. Reluctantly I do what seems the logical thing to do and politely refuse the drink he has to offer! Somehow I'm fairly sure I don't drink brandy anyway, but even if my mind is a bit fuzzy, it's clear enough to know that brandy certainly won't help me right now.

In my still confused state it seems logical to follow him. We have only gone just from sight of the road when he grabs my arm, turns me toward him and, with that same smirk on his face, says,

"Well Jenny girl, I reckon it's time you pay me for the lift."

Feeling a mixture of confusion and panic, all I can say is, "Sorry, I didn't know you wanted paying. I would gladly, but I'm afraid I haven't got any money on me at all."

"Money, who said anything about money. There's other ways to pay than money. I'm sure the likes of you must be used to paying for what you want, just like others pay you for what they want eh? Come on, don't play the innocent with me girl. Here have a swig of this, it'll put you in the mood," and as he says this he waves the brandy under my nose once more.

Before my mind could comprehend what was happening I find myself grabbed roughly by the arm, rammed hard up against the nearest tree, and trapped helplessly by my assailant, feeling terrified and unprepared to defend myself.

What can I do? I try to scream out for help but he stifles this first with his hand, then, finding other uses for his hand, replaces it with his mouth, stifling me with his awful bad breath.

I'm not sure what comes over me but, just as I'm admitting defeat and thinking all I can do is give in to his demands, I find something in me instinctively takes over, making me bring my knee up with an almighty thrust which takes him by surprise and sends him reeling in agony just for long enough for me to jump away and, adding a sharp kick to the groin for luck, rush off through the trees, hopefully out of sight of my aggressor.

With no idea where to run to all I can do is to put as much space between us as possible, as quickly as possible. Luckily this is a fairly thick wooded area with plenty of cover to hide in whilst I sort my clothing and regain something like composure and, to my great relief, see that I'm not being followed.

Listening carefully I can hear the sound of his HGV starting up. Obviously he thinks it's not worth the bother to pursue me thank goodness. I'm glad to sit myself down with my back to a tree to take a much needed rest. I can't help feeling shaken by the experience, but at the same time, quite proud of the way I managed to deal with it. Not knowing who I am I had no idea that I was capable of doing that.

Chapter Three.

I'm not sure how long I stayed here as I suddenly come to and realise I've been asleep again, but no idea for how long as I have no watch, and of course, I still have no identity!

Not daring to attempt any further hitch hiking I decide I must do my best to keep going on foot through the woods which appear to come out by the side of a smaller road headed for the town. I figure it's safer to keep at a discreet distance from the traffic until I'm closer to civilisation after my last experience.

Staying just inside the tree line I follow the direction of the traffic going my way, at least I hope this is my way. Though it's not ideal, I begin to wish I'd grabbed that flask of brandy before I ran. Anything liquid would surely be better than the parched throat I'm feeling right now. At least maybe I'd be too drunk to feel all the aches and pains that are setting in as I go! Those sounds I had heard earlier had certainly given a very false impression of the distance between where I was when I heard them and where the town actually is. On foot the road seems never ending!

Even so it is not so long before I come out of the woods and follow what must be a footpath, still heading in the same direction, but away from the traffic. I pass behind a small row of cottages, none of which I recognise.

Why can't I see something I recognise? Why is my mind such a blank? I don't understand why my surroundings seem so alien to me. I'm certain this is not a place I've been ever before, nothing like. If I had I'm sure I would remember something, especially bearing in mind that I reckon this looked the sort of place I would really like, under different circumstances. But, try as I might, I just can't put my finger on how I know all this, or if not from here, where do I come from and how did I get here? Even more importantly, how did I end up in that damn cave, and was that really an explosion I heard?

Anyway, I must have been walking for much longer than it seems. I suppose I'm not taking into account the couple of times I've slept since escaping my imprisonment in the cave I'd started from that morning. Though now I come to think of it perhaps, just because that was the first daylight I'd seen today, that may not even have been morning! With no way of telling the time how can I be sure?

Either way the sun is dropping fast in the sky and the air is turning decidedly fresh now. I really wish I knew where home was and could be tucked up in a warm, cosy bed. I don't know why but I feel reluctant to go back and knock on the door of any of the cottages I passed a few minutes ago. Perhaps I should find some shelter for the night and try approaching people in the morning. Aware of how I must appear it would be unlikely that anyone would appreciate me accosting them in the twilight. I wish I had something warmer to put on but all I'm wearing is this thin shirt. All I can do is roll down the sleeves and tuck my hands up inside the cuffs, making me look even sillier!

There's what looks like some sort of park up ahead so perhaps I can find shelter there for the night. As I pass a car parked under a street light I get the first glimpse of just what I do look like; my God, what a mess, now I know there's no way I can approach anyone looking like this. I look like a tramp. Perhaps I am! As if to confirm that thought a couple of kids, probably about twelve or so years old, seem to see me heading towards them and cross over the road as if to avoid me. Maybe I'm being too sensitive, but I can't help feeling really upset by this, though I don't really blame them for doing what I would do myself under the circumstances.

I can see some sort of building across the park a way, perhaps a shed, cricket pavilion or something. I so badly need it to be unlocked so I can find the shelter I need for the night. As I walk in that direction I see a man sat on a bench quite close to it and find myself hesitate before moving forward. Once again I'm faced with the dilemma of whether to ask for help, or whether, after my last encounter with an unknown man, this will be yet another risk, and so I wait and watch from a safe distance as he gets up from the bench he's been sitting on, throws his newspaper in the bin by the side of it, and strolls off in the opposite direction.

As soon as he's out of sight I make my way to what turns out to be a cricket pavilion as I'd thought. Desperate for shelter and a chance to hide away from the world for a few hours, I go straight to the door and try desperately to pull or prise it open, but with no luck. Having no success there I go round the building and try each window in turn, plus the door at the rear, but all without success. Now what? I'm so tired and cold, and this terrible feeling of desperation, the same one I'd felt back when I was trapped in the cave, was overtaking my senses. I need to sleep, I must sleep. If I don't find a way to close out the day and sleep until I'm ready to make some sort of sense out of everything and decide what to do next I think it'll drive me completely mad.

Perhaps I could curl up under a nearby bush? Seems not such a bad idea, at least it'll keep some of the wind away and keep me hidden from any passers-by, but just as I head toward it I can feel a few drops of rain against my face and I'm not sure about this idea. Though it's perhaps not so well hidden there is always the veranda on the pavilion. At least it will keep me fairly dry, and by chance, faces away from the worst of the wind. But I'm still so cold. What can I do to keep me just a bit warmer? Then I remember the newspaper that man put in the bin, I'll go and fetch it. It seems at least today must be a Sunday. Though it's too dark to read it, the size of the paper gives that away, so it will be better than nothing.

It's only now, when I curl up on the hard wooden veranda, cover myself the best I can with the well-thumbed paper, and resign myself to the protection of the dark, starless sky, that I feel the awful pangs of hunger and thirst take over my mind. Yet even these still seem insignificant compared to the ever constant and terrifying problems of where am I, why am I here and, even more worrying still, who am I?

Chapter Four.

What was that? Something hard hit me and brought me awake quite suddenly. As I sit up there's another hit, whack, it gets me squarely in the middle. Sure enough, by my side there's two pretty hefty chunks of turf, muddy ones at that, and straight in front of me with muddy hands, a group of three kids preparing another projectile and shouting "tramp, tramp, dirty old tramp!"

I'm pretty sure they're the same kids that crossed the road to avoid me last night. I suppose they can't be blamed for seeing me as a tramp, curled up here covered in an old newspaper. Even so, I feel upset by their attitude, and though part of me wants to burst into tears, another part of me is fuming that they should feel free to be so spiteful to one they assume is in this position. Whatever would their parents think of their behaviour I wonder, and what will I do if I get hold of them?

"Get out of here you lot and leave me alone. Don't you have school to go to or something? "

As I pull myself up to my feet and make to move in their direction they turn on their heels and rush off across the park. I probably hit the nail on the head reminding them they should be on their way to school, or perhaps they just didn't fancy hanging around to see what my reaction would be to their unwelcome wakeup call!

Other than them there seems to be no one else about. It's only now that I feel a burning thirst in my throat. What can I do? I don't reckon I ought to drink from the lake I can see a little way off. There are ducks and a couple of swans on and near the edge of it. It's probably a bit polluted. Instead, the only other thing I can do is to wet my hands on the leaves of trees around me and moisten my mouth from that.

I've got to work out what to do next, it's no good sitting around feeling sorry for myself. I must find answers to my three questions as soon as possible. Just how I don't know but I must stop hiding away, there must be help from somewhere. At least the rain has stopped and the sun is just poking its face over the horizon. An idea strikes me that perhaps I might learn something from the newspaper that had been my night covering. After all, it had been pretty useless as a blanket on the whole, so perhaps it might be more use in its original purpose as a source of information. I'll go and sit on the bench near the path and study it for clues.

Of course the first disappointment, which I had expected anyway, was that it wasn't a local but a national paper. That eliminates any answer to where I am. But looking around me at the nearby countryside and remembering that which I'd seen yesterday, it seems there's a good chance this is somewhere in the north, perhaps around the Pennines or Peak District area. Once again I can't imagine just how I've come to be here, and even less so, why that is. I'm sure I don't come from this area at all. Then of course there'll be no clue in a national newspaper as to my identity. This is my main worry, just not being able to put my finger on who I am. I seem to know who I'm not…I'm not Jenny, and I'm not from around here, but I'm pretty certain the reason for my memory loss has to do with the almighty crack on the head I can still feel. Perhaps my memory will come back if and when my head stops aching from that.

The headlines, in fact the first two pages, is really monotonous reading as it's taken up with different politicians ideas on the rights and wrongs of Brexit. Seems they're all determined to make it as difficult as possible! Though it all sounds familiar I'm not interested in any of it, I have too many problems of my own, and this is not one of them!

I soon decide I'm fed up with this. I can't imagine there's going to be much of interest in this rag after all, but just as I'm about to throw it back in the bin some of the inner pages fall to the ground. As I bend down to retrieve them my eye catches a picture of a girl with a heading beneath it reading, 'Woman wanted by police in connection with murder.'

No, it can't be, it does look like me, or at least the reflection of me I saw yesterday. But what's this about a murder, and what does it have to do with me? Now I really feel shaken to the core and panic stricken.

'The police are keen to find and interview a twenty-seven year old woman by the name of Melanie Cook, in connection with the death of a thirty-five year old business man in Surrey three days ago. She is around five foot four inches tall, slim build, and has long blonde hair. Anyone seeing her is asked to ring the police on telephone number 101.'

I feel completely dumbfounded by this. It can't be me, I might not know who I am but I can't possibly be a murderer, it's surely not meaning me! I must have a double or something. There again, if this happened in Surrey, how the hell did I get to be in a cave in this part of the country? A strange place that would have been to hide if I had needed to. I'm so bewildered and can't for the life of me think what to do next. If this murder happened three days ago that would be last Thursday, but surely I hadn't been in the cave that long even if my memory is still dodgy. No...this is wrong, there's got to be an explanation to all this.

On the other hand, if this is true, then I suppose at least I now have a name...Melanie Cook. Melanie, Mel, yes that feels right. That's who I am. I also know today must be Monday March 25th, at least that's if this is yesterday's paper, and have some idea which part of the country I suppose I come from, and a vague idea, going by the surrounding countryside, of which part I'm in now. Even so, where to go and what to do are probably my next priorities. Perhaps best to find the nearest police station and tell them this is all a mistake ... but would they believe me?

I'll head into town, partly to see if I either recognise anyone or anything, and partly to learn exactly where I am, that'll be a start. As I get up, fold the paper and put it back in the bin in which I'd found it, I notice a man wearing a sort of camouflage jacket leaning on a tree a few metres away. It seems to me he looked away when I looked in his direction, but perhaps it's my imagination. Yet as I start to walk away I can't help feeling I'm being followed. I daren't look round, so I just walk that bit faster. Panic begins to set in. I really do want to look but too scared to do so. If I had the courage perhaps I'd turn and challenge him but what would I say, and what would he do if I did? I'll pretend I've not noticed him and 'casually' walk off towards the park gates.

Ah, as I go through the gates I dare to glance over my shoulder and can't see any sign of him. There, I was just imagining things, I've got to pull myself together and stop being such a wimp. Just because someone is going anywhere near the same way as me it doesn't necessarily mean that they're after me.

Anyway, I must carry on down into town to see if I can find help of some sort. The town, so I gather from the pavilion and the sign on the park gate, is Chesterfield, and the name of the park appears to be Queens Park. Although I'm sure I must have heard the name Chesterfield before, I'm equally sure I've not actually been here. But then, I wonder, when I get there just what should I do? Where should I turn for help? I'm really not too sure about going to the police, they may not believe me. I have no proof of my innocence, come to that I can't be absolutely certain of it myself let alone convince them of it.

As I come into the outskirts of town I begin to pass people, probably many of them making their way to work. No one has time to look at me, thank goodness. Though I saw something of my appearance in the HGV mirror and the reflection in the car window I passed last night, after a night sleeping rough under a newspaper, I must look far worse. I'd give anything for a shower and a hair wash. That's the worst of having long hair, blonde at that. When it gets in a mess it looks really awful, and mine couldn't get in much worse mess than it feels right now! Perhaps, once again, that's why I feel people are avoiding looking at me, even avoiding walking too close.

Just then, as I'm daydreaming about my appearance and my situation, there's a sudden commotion right in front of me. A woman on a cycle who has just passed me is sent sprawling across the pavement by a car turning left in front of her! As I stand there watching folk from all around rush to her aid, I feel useless. I feel I should do something…ring for an ambulance or something, but of course I don't have a phone, and someone else is already doing it anyway. She seems to be unconscious and I hear someone say she shouldn't be moved until the paramedics have checked her over. One man moves her crushed cycle out of the road and directs traffic away from coming too close, while two women stay by her, gently putting a folded jacket under her head.

As I stand a short way off watching all this activity I'm suddenly aware of a figure of another man stroll by, casually picking up a rucksack from near the remains of the woman's bike. There's something familiar about him. Yes, of course, this is the same one I'd seen in the park, the one I'd thought was following me!

What should I do? Should I shout and draw people's attention to this thief? Before I get chance to do anything he walks up to me and, without a word, grabs me by the arm and pushes me unceremoniously round the side of the shop I'm standing by out of sight.

"Let me go, what the hell do you think you're doing? And how could you take that bag like that when the poor woman is lying there badly injured? Don't you have any scruples you …"

For the second time in as many days I find myself stopped mid flow by a firm hand over my mouth. For the second time I prepare to retaliate in the same way as before. But before I get chance to I see a look of mild amusement in the eyes in front of me, and hear a gentle voice that comes just in time to stop me fighting against what, after all, seemed not to be coming.

"Shhh, I'm not going to hurt you. I've been watching you, and I reckon you're new to this game, so thought I'd try and help. Of course, if you don't want any help I can clear off."

"New? New to what game? Anyway, who are you?"

"My name is Steve, what's yours?"

"I'm Mel…well I think I am, and anyway, that still hasn't told me what game you think I'm new to," I'm beginning to worry about just what 'game' he does reckon I am new to.

"Well hello Mel, it's nice to meet you. For goodness sake stop looking so scared will you, whatever do you think I'm going to do to you?"

"How do I know what you're going to do? Just let go of me or I'll…"

"You'll what? Scream? Run?"

I'm beginning to find his look of amusement at my expense more than a little annoying. Yet somehow I don't feel threatened by him in the slightest, which is strange knowing he's been watching and following me all morning. In fact now, as he lets go of my arm, I find myself making no attempt to take off as I had the previous day from the lorry driver, and actually found myself relieved to be with someone I just might be able to talk to.

Now I take the time to look properly at this Steve character, I have to admit, though purely to myself of course, that he's not a bad looking chap. I imagine a few years older than me, considerably taller, and with slightly wavy, dark hair (even though a little in need of a trim!), and a good covering of facial hair to match!

"Let's get out of here and go somewhere we can talk properly, before you draw too much attention to us!" and without checking to see I'm following he marches off back toward the park. Just like a small kid I find myself meekly trotting along behind him with no idea what else to do.

We didn't go to the bench where I'd sat earlier that day but another a little way distant and nearer the trees.

"Tell me first, just why you said you 'think' your name is Mel? Don't you know, or are you just trying to pretend you are not Mel?"

"No, it's nothing like that, anyway why should I want to pretend?" Once again I feel myself getting wound up by his attitude, and his cheek at questioning me.

"Ok, ok, don't get so touchy. Just thought it might be something to do with this," he says, pulling out of his pocket a piece of newspaper. To my surprise this is the cutting about me, or at least, who I believe to be me. He must have retrieved it from the bin after I put it in there.

I don't know what to say, how to answer him. After all I have no answers to give myself let alone him. All I can do is snatch it from him and screw it up which, on reflection really serves no purpose. But then nothing was serving any purpose just now, and all I want to do is run away and hide from him and the rest of the world. Perhaps I should have stayed locked away in that awful dark cave. Struggling to fight back the tears I feel trickling slowly down I go to get up and leave before he sees them, but he puts a hand on my arm and urges me to sit back down.

"I'm sorry, I don't mean to upset you. I just thought you might need someone to talk to about whatever this is.

Please don't go, or at least not until you know where to go to, or what to do next. Things are seldom as bad as they seem and I bet there's a simple explanation for it all."

"I don't know, I don't know anything anymore…I don't even know who I am for sure, or how I got to be here, and I certainly don't know what to do about it," at which point I just can't hold the tears back any longer, and find myself crying like a baby on a park bench, with the arm of a man I met less than an hour ago round my shoulder!

Chapter Five.

By the time I manage to stop myself blubbing like a baby I realise I've gone from just having his arm round my shoulder to burying my face in his chest, therefore leaving a large wet patch on his shirt (a none too fresh shirt at that!). I try to apologise but he says it's ok.

"Now you've got all that out the way how about you wiping your eyes, blowing your nose and talking sensibly about whatever your problem is? After all, you're not the only one living out here on the streets you know."

Just for a second I stare at him in bewilderment before fully taking in the implications of his assumption.

"But I'm not living on the streets, or at least I don't think so. At least I don't think I am."

Steve throws me another one of his slightly amused grins before once again asking what I mean by that. "You really don't seem to know much about yourself do you? Well then, how about starting with what you do know?"

"That's just it, I genuinely don't know much. I really can't remember much at all and it's scary. All I think I know is that I believe somehow at some time I've had a hell of a bash on the head! You can still feel a lump here, on my head." I pushed my hair back to point this out to him.

Steve ran his hand over my head and was quite surprised at the size of the lump there. "Ouch! You're certainly right about that, and you say you really don't know how that happened? Did someone hit you, or did you just bump it do you reckon?"

As we sit there on the bench I calm my mind to the best of my ability, trying hard to stem the feelings of panic that occasionally sweep over me and, going back as far as my mind will allow, tell him everything I can remember beginning with when I came to in the cave.

"So you really don't remember anything from before that then? It's certainly a weird story. I can't imagine you'd have just wandered into a cave and bashed your head hard enough to cause a bump like that, and certainly not enough to cause the memory loss you've got. So do you reckon you are this Mel woman that the cops are looking for?

"I tell you I don't know! Mind you, I think that is my name, sounds familiar, but whoever I am I'm sure I had nothing to do with any murder." As I look up at him I'm relieved to see he looks as if he believes me on that count. "I just don't know what to do next though. Perhaps best just to hand myself in to the police and let them sort it out for me."

"Hold on a bit, that might not be such a good idea right now with no proof and being so vague about everything. If they have reason to think you're worth looking for, they must have something to go on, some evidence of some sort. No, your best bet is to keep your head down until your memory sorts itself out and we can find proof you're not involved."

"By 'we' do you mean you might help me? Where would we start?" and then an even more pressing thought comes to mind, "I don't suppose you've got any money on you so we could get something to eat, I'm starving and not eaten since…I really can't remember when, and I'd kill for a drink right now?"

There's that annoying grin again looking at me, and that sarcastic voice saying, "Perhaps not the best choice of words under the circumstances."

I'd not realised just what I'd said, but I suppose he's right.

"So what does madam require? A three course lunch? Be sensible now, you might not have been used to living on the streets but I've been doing it now for a few years. No, out here you have to use your initiative or starve I'm afraid. Why do you think I grabbed that bag?"

As he says this he picks up the rucksack from under the bench and opens it up to examine the contents. "No, food wise the best she's got in here is a packet of chewing gum, probably not quite what you had in mind." Then looking into the purse he finds inside, "Aha, that's more like it, probably enough to buy a couple helpings of fish and chips and a cuppa, if that's to your liking of course madam?"

"Will you stop being so sarcastic and point me in the direction of the food," I tell him, but before he agrees to do so Steve stops and looks me up and down as if I'm being inspected. "Now what? I know I'm a mess but I can't help that, and you're not that fresh looking yourself anyway!"

"No it's not that. We need to see no one recognises you from the description in the paper. That long blonde hair, well it was blonde no doubt when it was clean, is a bit of a giveaway. Let's have another rummage in here," he says, picking up the rucksack again. "Ah, think we're in luck again."

To my absolute horror he produces a pair of nail scissors from a manicure set! "You don't really expect to cut it with those do you? You must be kidding me! I don't want to cut it at all, let alone hack at it with a pair of damn nail scissors."

"Ok, please yourself. Only trying to help. With that attitude you might as well hand yourself over to the police now to save their time looking for you. Now, do you want that food or not?"

Reluctantly, as I can't see any way out of it, I submit to his less than expert ministering with the scissors, seeing my (what should be) beautiful long locks fall on the ground around us. When he finishes he gives me a compact from the bag so that I can take a squint at his (not so) handy work. What a sight! At this point, to add insult to injury, he dives once more into the bag and comes out with a blue beanie, which he insists I should put on.

"Just as a precaution, to cover up the colour, or at least the colour it should be," he adds with a laugh.

"You really know how to make a girl feel special don't you," I say hitting him round the head with it before pulling it over my own head. I must agree that my hair did feel pretty awful, but I'm not about to admit this to Steve.

"Ok, that's more like it. No one will give you a second glance looking like that," he says, and before I get chance to vent my anger at his insults he adds, "Now shall we go get some food?"

It doesn't take me much decision making to decide which to do, tear into him for his bad manners, or once again trot after him in the same childlike fashion as before. My hunger is so great that right now food has to override anything else, so I'll have to overlook his manners for now.

We must look a right scruffy pair as we walk back into town together. I can't help catching a glimpse of our reflection in a shop window as we go and can see why Steve thought I'm another homeless soul like him, especially with my scruffy bits of rough cut hair sticking out from under this silly hat. I'd hate to admit it but he was right to suggest it though. Right now I don't care what I look like as long as I get to eat as I reckon I can't have eaten for ages, possibly days for all I know. It's strange to think I have absolutely no idea when I did last eat. We'd not gone far before coming to a little fish and chip shop into which Steve leads me, and without saying a word he sat me at a table in a quiet corner before going and ordering fish, chips and mushy peas twice, once again assuming he knew what I liked best!

I must look like a ravenous dog the way I attack this feast. I'm sure a humble plate of fish and chips has never tasted so good! We washed it down as we ate with cups of tea, once again like nectar to the gods as far as I'm concerned. There are only two other couples in the place, both sitting a little way off, perhaps preferring not to mix with such as us. Up on the wall in the corner there is a television going for the benefit of the customers, though I don't think anyone is taking a bit of notice of it. Come to that neither are we really. Or at least, certainly not at first while food is our priority.

Even so, I'm suddenly dug in the ribs by Steve, and before I get chance to object, find him surreptitiously jerking his head in the direction of the tv. I'm about to ask why when I realise he's trying to draw my attention to a story on the national news. I've obviously missed most of it, and the rest has to rely on how fast we can read the subtitles as the sound is right down, but I get the gist of it.

"since the discovery of the body of Mr Jake Marden in his Surrey home on Thursday last. Meanwhile the police are still keen to interview his twenty-seven year old fiancée, Melanie Cook, in connection with his death. She has not been seen since the event, but was believed to have been in the house the previous day."

One minute I'm looking into the face of a man I know I'm close to, the next it's replaced with a face I now know to be mine! Jake…yes of course I know Jake. My mind is suddenly a swirl of mixed thoughts, mixed emotions. I feel as if it will either burst or I'll just pass out where I sit. I start to gabble a rush of unanswerable questions, not really at anyone in particular, most probably at myself. Before I can draw attention to myself I find Steve grabbing me by the arm and marching me briskly out the door, up a side street and into a quiet alley behind the shops.

"Pull yourself together before you get us both arrested," he says firmly.

"I'm sorry," I say, "but I've just realised that it really is me they're looking for. I know that now because I recognise Jake. He can't be dead, that can't be true surely? What do they mean about him being murdered? I'm sure he was ok last time I saw him. Why would anybody do that? Who would do that to Jake?"

So many questions and no answers are rushing at me all at once, and once again I feel my head swirl, my knees fold, and then…nothing!

Chapter Six.

When the black curtain lifts from my eyes I find myself lying on the ground in what I believe is called the recovery position. Under my head is a recognisable aroma of Steve's jacket spread over the rucksack. I have to own up to feeling relieved to know he is still around, though it's pretty well dusk and I can't see him right now. As I sit myself up I hear footsteps coming toward me, perhaps that's him, so I call out to him quietly,

"Is that you? Where've you been? What's happened?"

But the voice I hear is definitely not Steve. In fact there are three of them looming up out of the shadows. As they come close to me it's clear they are either drunk or on drugs, maybe even both going by the slurred speech. I want to get up and run but find myself surrounded by them.

"Hello little lady," says the biggest one, bending down much to close for comfort to me, "You look as if you need more of what you've already had. I'm sure we can spare you a bit if you've got the cash?"

"No, I don't do drugs thanks. Leave me alone."

"Oh now, don't be like that, you look ready for a bit more. You'd feel so much more sociable with a bit more you know," and as he said that they all begin to close in on me at once. "Let's have a look in that bag and see what you've got in there."

Now what do I do? I may have just about coped with that one lorry driver, but I feel totally defenceless against these three. I try to call for Steve but my mouth is too dry, nothing comes out. As they close in on me I grab the bag and try to get to my feet, but the big chap pushes me back down. I know I haven't a chance of defending myself against him, let alone all three, but just as I'm desperately looking for a way to make a quick getaway I'm relieved to hear a familiar voice from behind them,

"Back off you lot, leave her alone and try picking on someone your own size."

Steve steps out from the shadows, pushes the smaller one out of the way, and puts himself between me and them. For a split second they stare at him as if he's from another planet, before the big one eyes him up and down and, with a grin to his mates which clearly says 'who does this fool think he is?', looks Steve in the eye and asks, "Why, what are you going to do about it tramp?"

"Let the girl go and I'll show you," and taking the big man's grin as his answer, turns to me and handing me the bag says quietly, "Go back to where we were earlier…go on, go."

The last thing I want to do is leave him at the mercy of this gang on his own, but something in his tone of voice tells me not to argue, so I do as he says and take off into the darkness with the bag. I assume he meant to go back to the park, why I don't know. How will he get away from them or even survive any sort of fight with three against one?

Reluctantly I find my way back to the bench and sit there nervously waiting. Have I done the right thing leaving Steve? What should I have done? Stayed and backed him up? But I don't reckon I'm much of a fighter. Perhaps I should have called the police. But then we might all have been arrested, the druggies for what they had on them, Steve for assisting an offender, and me by all accounts for murder! I'll go back and see what's happened, see if I can at least try to help him.

As I walk toward the gate of the park I find a sizeable stick on the ground under a tree. I'll take that to defend myself. As I approach the alley where I left Steve I hear footsteps coming toward me. I hold the stick up ready to strike whoever is coming,

"Whoa! Careful what you're doing with that weapon," and I'm much relieved once more to find its Steve's slightly light hearted voice attached to the footsteps.

"Are you ok? What happened? Where have they gone?" my questions come thick and fast, but bearing in mind the situation he was in last time I saw him, is that surprising? He doesn't look as if he has a scratch on him, yet I can't believe they just walked away so easily. As he brushes himself off I see a broad grin come over his face as he nods his head in the direction he'd just come from,

"Oh them," as if I'd be asking about anyone else, "they're in there where the rubbish belongs."

I look in the direction he's pointing to see one of those big rubbish bins shops use to put their outdated food in!

"What? Do you mean you've put them in that bin?" As I ask this I timidly lift the lid just far enough to see three prone bodies in a squirming mass in the bottom of it. "How the hell did you do that? There was three of them and only one of you!"

"That'd be telling. Have you still got the bag? Good, now let's get away from here before anyone sees us. We need to get under cover before it gets any colder, but first we need to get you cleaned up and that hair sorted out."

"I thought we'd already done that with those damned scissors? Wasn't that good enough for you? What more mess do you have in mind?"

Without bothering to answer me Steve fishes in the bag once more and takes out the purse. I'm really uncomfortable with us making free with the poor woman's belongings, but it seems Steve has no such scruples. He hands me a ten pound note, and as we head toward the end of the street he points me in the direction of a chemist shop and instructs me to go and buy myself some hair dye,

"Keep your hat well down over your hair, and don't get any of these stupid red, blue or purple ones. Just an average dark brown."

So once again off I trot like an obedient child! Why do I keep doing this? Probably because I already feel I can trust him and, let's face it, who else have I got? I choose dark brown as I was instructed and the girl behind the counter takes little or no notice of me when I go to pay as she's busy stacking boxes of toiletries on the shelf by the till and speaking to someone on the end of her mobile at the same time as she takes my money.

When I get outside Steve is waiting for me and ushers me away into the darkness and toward the park once more. "This is all very well but how am I supposed to use this? You do know it has to be put in, left for a while, and then washed out?"

"Don't you worry about that, I've got all that sorted," and so saying I find myself marched off briskly in the direction of the park once more! When we get inside the gate he asks me how much change I have left from the tenner I used for the dye. There is about three pounds. He gives me another couple 'just in case', and hands me the rucksack. "Inside this there's a pair of jeans and a clean jumper, and probably a few other useful looking things…looks like our poor lady was heading this way anyway at some point. Anyway, I want you to go in, pay as if you're going for a swim, then dive in the showers and dye your hair. When you've done that you can put the clean clothes on too."

Well, he's certainly well organised, or should I say he's certainly got me well organised! I must say that the thought of getting under a hot shower sounds so good I'm not about to argue, so I obediently take the bag from him and, keeping my head down, head for the door of the leisure centre. "I'll be quite a while though, "Where will you be when I come out?" I ask before going in.

"Don't worry, I'll be just inside the door when you've finished. Take your time and enjoy it while you've got chance. Go on, go."

A slight hesitation, then I'm on my way in. Once again I'm hoping nobody looks too closely at me, but I needn't worry, the ladies behind the desk seem to be arguing about something and hardly look up as I just say I want to swim, pick up the ticket one of them pushes at me, and walk on passed as if I knew exactly where to go. Luckily it was quite well signposted to the ladies changing room. It's not until I get there I realise I have clean jeans and jumper, but don't have essentials such as a towel, and more importantly, clean underclothes! Now what to do? I think I already know Steve well enough to know just what he would say; he'd tell me to improvise! I look around the empty cubicles but I'm just about to give up as it seems most people are good and put their things in lockers, when I find there is a bigger communal changing room where a few had changed and left things on the benches.

At last I'm in luck, I manage to find a good dry towel on one heap, and from another, though I'm reluctant to do so, a really nice, clean set of underwear of about my size, obviously brought in preparation for use after her swim. I do feel rather guilty, but I tell myself that she still has the set she came in and that my need is greater than hers on this occasion! I consider leaving my old, dirty ones as a replacement, but I really can't imagine she'd appreciate that, and anyway, it might risk incriminating me in theft as well as murder!

Wanting to get finished and out before anyone comes back, I dash into a shower cubicle with my newly acquired gear. Luckily there's room to keep the dry things hanging at a safe distance from the shower, so I strip off and comb the colour through my hair. While it's taking I manage to stand most of my body under the hot water, and when I've given it time to take, I rinse my hair off, pleased to stick my head under the gorgeously hot water. Ahh, it feels amazing. I could stand here for ages. But no, I must get on with the job in hand. All I hope is that it works well, and that by standing the remains of my body under the hot water while it takes, I didn't dye myself dark brown all over! I hadn't realised until I'd read the instructions that I'd need to leave it on for so long, but it seems I'm in luck as the ladies whose things I've helped myself to are just starting an aqua-fit class, and so would be gone for some time.

Eventually, having rinsed out my hair and dried myself I reluctantly and with a little trepidation, pop my head out of the shower fully dressed in lovely clean clothes and head for the door, but before reaching it I see myself in a mirror and realise that, though the colour is fine, my wet hair is a mess. Next to the mirror I find hair dryers and, remembering seeing a small brush in the bag, stop just long enough to do a quick blow dry. It really doesn't take so much with so little hair, in fact I even trim a few odd strands to tidy it up before leaving.

45

Once again nobody is paying any attention to me as I approach the door, and I'm so relieved to see Steve standing just inside waiting for me. I'm even more pleased when he hands me a coffee he's obviously bought from the drinks machine nearby.

"Thought now you've warmed up the outside you might like to warm the inside a bit too. Guessed you wouldn't want sugar?"

"Good guess, thanks. This is just what I need. Well...What do you think of the new look," I ask, giving him a quick twirl.

"Perfect, but don't make a show of yourself, you're not supposed to be seen, remember. By the way, where did you put your old gear? I meant to warn you not to leave them there."

"Just as well I didn't then," I tell him in a rather smug tone, "I washed them out and put them in a big polythene bag I found. Thought I might need them later."

"Come on then, let's get out of here." And then, looking at me as a shiver runs through my body as the cool evening air hits me says, "Why didn't you find yourself a coat of some sort while you were about it," and as he says this putting his own jacket round my shoulders.

There, just as I was priding myself of getting things right I find I've still not quite managed it. Somehow I feel suitably reprimanded for my lack of forethought!

Chapter Seven.

"Where are we going?" I ask as we walk away from the leisure centre and out of the park gates still drinking our amazingly hot coffee.

"Somewhere out of the cold, or at least out of the worst of it, and somewhere we can get some rest. Then in the morning I think we'd better have a frank discussion as to just what your story really is, don't you?" I must have looked more than a little worried at the prospect of this, but Steve was quick to add that I mustn't worry any more tonight, "Your memory seems to be creeping back slowly, so you just need to let it come in its own time. The more you stress over it, the worse it'll be."

"That's easy for you to say but I bet you've never been through anything as stressful as this, I bet your life's been a doddle," I throw at him.

His reaction to this remark was sudden, unexpected and for a split second, verging on violent as he spun round to face me with a look of pure rage, and shouted,

"Don't you dare say that! You've no idea what stress is!"

I stopped dead in my tracks, not knowing what I'd said that was so wrong. Should I apologise or turn and run, would either help, so I just waited for his reaction…there wasn't one. In the next split second he just turned and walked on beckoning me to follow.

Up until this point I must say that Steve had from the start, well, almost the start, given me no reason to think he might be any danger to me. Yet I can't help thinking now just how easily he seemed to deal with those three druggies single-handed. There was obviously more to this man than your average homeless tramp. Perhaps I should try to find out, but I think, going by the sudden flash of temper I'd just witnessed, maybe I'd be best not to pry. Perhaps I'd find out more later, but until then I think I'll keep out of his business and just hope I'm as safe with him as he's made me feel up until now. After all, right now he's all I've got.

I want to ask where we're going to spend the night but hardly dare open my mouth, so I do just follow as I'm bid, once again feeling childish and inadequate. I wonder if the real me really is this useless or is it all because of the bash on the head I've had? Perhaps he's right and things will look better after a night's sleep, but where is he taking me for this, and is sleep all he has in mind?

Oh, for goodness sake, why the hell should I even suspect him of anything untoward? Other than the one flash of temper just now, and his way of gaining satisfaction at annoying me with that wry grin at my expense, he's shown no interest in me in that way.

We've not walked so far when we came to the allotments I'd passed yesterday. I want to make some cheeky remark about 'surely we're not going gardening,' but still can't bring myself to speak, so follow him toward a large shed on the plot near the back of the place, and to my surprise he opens the door and ushers me in.

"Don't look so worried, the old fellow that rents this plot barely uses it now. I've got to know him quite well, and knowing how I'm fixed he's happy for me to use it as my base. I pay him off sometimes with a bit of digging when he finds it too hard." As he says this he turns on a camping light of some sort, battery I think, then turns to me to say something, but stops whatever he was about to say and his gaze drops to the floor for an instant. "Look Mel...I'm sorry, I can see I've upset you. I didn't mean to, believe me. You just hit a sore spot. Please don't judge me by one stupid comment. Perhaps one day I'll be able to explain, but I promise I wouldn't hurt you and until then can you just take my word that I'm perfectly harmless?"

"Ok, but as for being 'perfectly harmless' I doubt those three druggies would agree with that!" As I said that it seemed to have the effect of taking us to a much more relaxed atmosphere, even sharing a laugh at their expense. What a relief I feel, as if a great weight had been lifted from me.

I watch as he rummages amongst a much bigger rucksack in the corner of the shed and produces a length of string which he fixes across one end of the shed. Having done this he tells me to hang my washing on here to dry, promising (with a laugh in his voice) not to look at my smalls. As I am doing this he reaches once more into this bag and comes out with a couple of rather tatty sleeping bags. These he spreads on an equally tatty looking groundsheet then, looking over his shoulder at me says, "Come on, wriggle in and get yourself comfy while you still feel a bit warm from the coffee and the walk here. Floor's a bit hard if you're used to luxury, but it's better than that cold veranda you slept on last night."

"So I was right, you were watching me? I knew someone was. Why didn't you help me then?"

There, much to my relief, in place of the rage he'd shown me earlier was that same wry grin I was beginning to become accustom to as he said, "Well, I didn't want to risk getting attacked by this strange woman, and going by the way you dealt with those kids, I reckon I made the right choice! Anyway, would you have trusted me, a strange man, suggesting you come to sleep in a shed with me, at that time of night? Now, get in there and get some sleep."

Without so much as another word I did as I was told.

Chapter Eight.

I came to with a start. What was that noise? I roll over and look around me. Where am I, and why am I here, who am…? No, no, no …stop it, I can't go through that again. Stop panicking and calm myself. Yes, I know who I am. I'm Melanie Cook. As for where I am, yes, of course I know; I'm here in a sleeping bag, in a shed with a man called Steve who I've known for all of twenty-four hours! What's wrong with that after all? As for why, the answer is simple; I'm being accused of my Jake's murder and I have no idea what else to do.

By my side there's an empty sleeping bag, obviously his, but no sign of its occupant. Where is he, I can't see him anywhere? Surely he hasn't gone and just left me lying here. No, I think I can hear him coming, or at least I hope it is him this time.

"You're awake then sleepy head. How're you feeling this morning?" As he comes in through the door I see he has a small pan of water in his hand. I watch as he puts a light to a little gas burner and puts the can on to it to heat up. "Soon have a hot drink to get you going. Sorry the breakfast menu isn't up to much, a boiled egg or nothing, I'm afraid it's the chef's day off today, but then come to think of it it's his day off most days!"

"Where did you get the eggs?" I ask, and of course I should have guessed there was a good answer to that question.

"Can't you hear the hens in the next door allotment?"

"I suppose that belongs to another mate of yours?" but this time I don't quite get the answer I'm expecting.

"No, never spoken to the man, but he has no idea how many eggs they lay, so he never misses the odd one, or two now you're here."

Is there no end to this man's cheek? He certainly knows how to survive living rough. I'm pretty sure I wouldn't survive this life long on my own. "So what do we do next?" I ask him.

"Well, first we drink this," as he hands me a steaming hot cup of tea, "then we eat our eggs. Then after that we talk."

"What do we talk about?" even as I ask knowing this is probably a stupid question. I can tell by the look he throws my way that it's me he wants us to talk about. I get in first by reminding him that, though he says his name is Steve, I don't even have a surname for him.

"Didn't I say? Sorry. Steve Lockett at your service ma'am. Do you feel happier now you know that?" I think he's mocking me, but in a way it does make me feel a little safer, goodness knows why!

As I sip my hot tea, I watch him carefully peel me one of the eggs and hand it to me with a slice of slightly dry bread on a tin plate from his bag, and we sit quietly with mugs in one hand, dry bread and eggs in the other, until 'breakfast' is over and the mugs and plates are rinsed off with the remains of the water from the can, at which time Steve sits back down by my side and says, "right, now I want you to think hard and tell me everything you remember this morning."

"I don't know what to say, all I can remember is that my name is Melanie Cook, and I am…was, engaged to Jake. I really don't know how I got here, nor do I know anything about him being murdered. But I'm sure I didn't kill him, I wouldn't do that, I really wouldn't, I …I …couldn't do that…" I can feel myself going into meltdown again even at the thought of it.

"Calm down, calm down, I don't believe for a minute you'd be capable of that. Now just calm yourself down and let's see if we can find anything coming out of there," he says tapping me gently on the head, "anything that might throw light on the whole situation."

Somehow his tone of voice begins to have the desired effect on my churned up mind. I try to think back, to visualise Jake, to picture where we were last time I'd seen him. "I'm not sure I can remember, it's all a bit of a blur. Why won't it come back to me?"

"Don't push yourself, it will in time, but if you try too hard your mind will block it all out. Just let it take its time and fill me in if and when you do think of anything." As he says this he gets up and stares out of the window, appearing to be in deep contemplation of his own for a few minutes. I can't help watching him for a brief moment thinking just what hidden depths of his own are hidden behind that capable, confident and independent façade he presents to the world. Once again though I chose not to delve.

I'm just rolling up the sleeping bag, assuming it goes back in his bag, as he turns and with a laugh in his voice says, "Oh, that's what I like to see, a woman who knows her place and tidies up!"

I'm about to give a sharp retort to that remark when something stops me in my tracks. A quick memory flashes across my mind making me stop almost before I get a word out. "I've just remembered something, or at least I think I have." Steve comes over to me and says to take my time and let it come, not to force it. "We had a row… Jake and I, something about him not tidying up after himself. I remember shouting at him and walking out."

"That's good, now do you remember when this was and where you walked out of. Just close your eyes and try to think about what you said. See if you can visualise where you were Mel."

"I'm not sure…a house, I think his house, quite a big one. It had red curtains on French doors, I went out of them and ran across a lawn. Do you think this means I did kill him?"

"What, for not tidying up? I doubt it. Can you remember where the house is? Did he come after you, or was there anyone else around at the time who would have seen what happened?"

54

"Well, the news said his home was in Surrey but I can't remember where about in Surrey. But yes, I think he did come after me. I think I remember him call my name. I don't remember anyone else being there, but it's all a bit hazy, but for some reason I think that was when something happened to me then because my mind seems a total blank from then until I woke up in the cave."

"Don't worry, it's coming back gradually. Just tell me any little thing that comes back to you and we can put it all in context as we go."

"What do you mean as we go, go where?" I feel I'm about to be railroaded into something but no idea what he has in mind.

"That I'm not quite sure of right now, but you're a hell of a way from Surrey here, and it seems to me we need to get a lot closer if we stand a chance of proving your innocence." As he says this he is rolling up his own sleeping bag and stuffing it in the rucksack along with mine and all the rest of the equipment we'd been using. I sit in silence watching him and mulling over what he's saying before coming out with the obvious questions,

"Hang on a minute… you're saying 'we' need to get closer, and 'we' need to prove my innocence. Do you mean you're going to help me, and you'll come to Surrey with me? Why would you do that?"

"Well somehow I don't think you'd get on too well on your own would you, and besides, I don't have anything better to do, I'm not exactly rushed off my feet with work right now am I?" He glances around the shed to see everything is packed away, then throws an order (or that's what it sounds like) to me to change back into my tatty looking clothes.

"And while you're at it just check to see if there's anything useful left in the other bag."

"Why can't I keep these jeans on, they're much better, and wouldn't it be a good idea to take that rucksack too?

"Brilliant idea; let yourself be seen walking around in that woman's clothes and carrying her bag. How far do you think you'd get before someone recognises them? By now she'd have reported them missing wouldn't she?"

I hadn't thought of that before but now he says that it's pretty obvious I suppose. Seems I've certainly got a lot to learn, but at least it seems I've got a good teacher. Reluctantly I gather up the still slightly damp things from the makeshift line. Steve tells me he'll leave me to it for a while as he's seen the old man arrive to dig a few spuds from the allotment, giving me chance to change in privacy. I can't help watching through the little window whilst I change. I hope I don't get in trouble when he comes in as I decide that even if I can't wear these better things now, perhaps I can take them for later! I watch as Steve helps the old chap dig up his spuds, then they chat for a while before shaking hands, then he comes back in.

"Just told old Bill I'm going away for a while, then I've got somewhere to come back to when I'm ready."

"Does he know I'm here?" I ask, but Steve gives a sharp intake of breath and shakes his head,

"Goodness me no! Poor old Bill would be horrified if he knew I'd spent the night in his she'd with a woman!"

It was good to find we were both sharing another good laugh, even if it was at the expense of the elderly gentleman.

Before we leave Steve insists on checking to see just what I've put in his bag. Obviously he isn't keen on the idea of me poking around amongst his personal stuff in the bottom, but I assure him I didn't invade his privacy! He seems ok about me keeping the clothes, as long as I don't get any of them out on display whilst we're in the area. I mention that I thought there was still the purse with a couple of notes, one ten and one five and some odd coins. "And I could swear there was a debit card in there last night," I tell him, "I had thought we could have made use of it before we leave."

"No, that would be worse than using her bag. You wouldn't be able to use a cash machine without her PIN, and even if you did know it, or try using it in a shop during daylight there are cctv cameras everywhere. That's why I've got rid of it."

"Oh ok, I see what you mean," then realising what he'd just said I asked, "What do you mean, got rid of it? When did you do that?"

"Oh that was last night while you were doing your hair and showering. I saw it in there when I gave you money to get in the centre, so I strolled back down, drew out some cash from a machine which was in a pretty dark area, not too visible from the cameras, then shoved it and the PIN in that skip. "

"What, you mean where those men were? And anyway, how did you know what the PIN was?"

"Wasn't too hard to guess. Her driving licence was in there with her date of birth, so I took a chance and tried that. That's a fatal mistake people make, keeping things like that in the same purse. So I just scribbled it on a piece of paper and shoved that with the card in that big chap's pocket and dropped the purse in separately!" He seemed to find that rather amusing.

"But suppose they found it and told the police that it was you who put it in there?"

"What, and miss the chance of a free fix? No way. They'll not be able to resist using it and I reckon that, by the time the police check who has used it they'll be as high as kites again. Should keep them off our tails I reckon. Anyway, we can keep the cash, but need to get rid of the bag, it's too identifiable. There's someone over the other side of the allotments got a bonfire going well. He's put plenty of wood and all sorts of junk on it, so he won't notice a bit more. Then we'll go back into town. There's some public toilets there. I sometimes go there for a trim and freshen up."

I look up at him a little surprised at the thought of him having a 'trim up'. How you do that with the facial hair that he sported was a puzzle to me, but I suppose he must keep it in trim as it was by no means long. I have to admit I would enjoy chance to throw some hot water over my face, so away we go, heading once more into town. I hope we will see nothing more of those three from last night, but I needn't worry. It was still fairly early in the morning and I doubt they would be around this time of day. In fact, I wonder if they're still in the skip! Even if they were about I can't see them fancying another dose of Steve!

Just for an instant when I remerge from my ablutions I can't see him anywhere. I know I must stay calm or I'll attract attention, but hardly a minute goes by when I see him sauntering toward me looking fresh and extremely well-trimmed. "What next," I ask him, "How do we get to Surrey from here?"

"We don't," he says to my surprise, "we just work our way nearer and see what we can find out without being found by the cops. We need to keep an eye on the news bulletins and papers. You can't just rock up and expect them to believe you without finding out just what did happen."

"You did," I say, to which I get just the sort of sarcastic reply I've come to expect,

"But I've seen enough of you already to know you haven't got the intelligence or ability to do it and get away with it!"

Chapter Nine.

It seems that before we head south Steve has decided we should go back to that awful cave. I can't see the point, and to be honest the thought makes me cringe, but he has some idea there might be some clue there as to how I got to be in such a place. He's pretty sure someone must have put me in there for whatever reason, so any clue might be valuable. I tell him the direction I'd taken to get here and, leaving out the full details of the incident with the lorry driver, explained I'd hitched a lift part of the way. "That's brave of you doing that when you're on your own. There's some dodgy characters out there you know."

Didn't I just know that, it's firmly embedded on my mind still? At least this time I'm not on my own. Just as well as there's no way I'd go back there alone anyway. Just what he thinks he can learn from a pile of rock I really don't know, but I've either got to go with him or take my chances on my own, not much of a choice eh?

Along the main road some way from where I'd been picked up yesterday we did manage to get the offer of a lift from a chap in a delivery van. Steve made a point of getting in first so that he was between the driver and myself, a thing I was glad of.

"Are you going far mate," the driver asked, to which Steve was quick to answer that we were just going to spend a while hill walking. "Your idea or your girlfriend's?" he asks.

Steve, without hesitation, explains that I'm not his girlfriend, I'm his sister and we've just recently lost our mother, which is why we thought a bit of time away might help us cope with the grief! What a hell of an imagination this man's got?

"Sorry to hear that," the driver says, "my name's Norman by the way.

Once again without hesitation, Steve says, "Sorry, I forgot to say, I'm Dave and her name is…" before he could say I heard myself say, "Jenny."

Eventually, with me nudging Steve to signal it to him, we reached as close as he was going to our destination. We thanked Norman and marched off across the open countryside, in the direction of the hills I'd come from yesterday. It seems that we are not so very far from caves in the Buxton area of the Peak district. We'd not gone far when he took hold of my arm, looked me in the eye and asked,

"Where did that come from …Jenny I mean, I thought you'd decided you were Mel?"

"I don't know, but I think I must know a Jenny because I told someone that yesterday. Shouldn't I have said that?"

To my relief Steve seems to approve of the idea that I should have a name different from my own, at least as far as strangers were concerned. He also seems quite impressed that I remember the direction I had taken up over the hill and toward the mouth of the cave. How could I forget it, the very thought of my struggle to escape from there makes me shiver. This involuntary action is not missed by him.

"Don't look so scared, I'm not expecting you to go back in there. All I want you to do is tell me everything you remember about what happened inside and what you remember about the layout of it. Then you can lie back and enjoy the rest. Might not get much later depending on where we go from here."

"You don't seriously intend to go inside there do you? Are you completely mad?" I ask him. "It's not safe, I'm sure there was some sort of explosion at one point."

"That's just why I do want to go in. Perhaps there might be some sort of clue as to why you ended up there, and if there was an explosion, any clue as to who was behind it." As he said this he put down the rucksack and rummaged down into it and coming out with a torch. "Now just think carefully and tell me all you remember about the inside of this cave."

Though that's not much to go on I try to explain what I do remember. The awful noise I heard, and the feel of the ground shaking around me. The sore head as I came too after what must have been a blackout, and the painful scramble through the sharp, rocky passages. I find myself shaking with the memories of it all. I'm trying to be strong but don't think I'm fooling myself let alone Steve. He sits back down by my side and puts a reassuring arm round my shoulders,

"Ok, don't let it upset you, it's over now, you're out and don't need to go back there again. Just you sit back and rest, I'll be back before you know it."

So saying he gets up, walks to the entrance, and vanishes into the dark mouth of the cave. All I can do is sit here and wait, though not so sure I'd call it rest, until to my great relief he emerges from the dark gaping mouth from whence I'd escaped previously. The serious expression on his face tells me he has found something, but seeing my worried expression this quickly turns to a smile.

"Well, you were right about hearing a bit of a bang. That would have been enough to bring the whole roof down if they'd known how to do it properly. Rough guess that's just what they were planning to do. Whoever did that never meant you to get out of there."

"Thank God they didn't know how to do it. What you're saying is that they put me in there to die? "

I cringe at the very thought of this, and feel truly thankful, knowing this, that Steve is now back safely, wondering at the same time just what I would do right now if he hadn't come out. As it is I'm still none the wiser as to who 'they' are who were responsible for my imprisonment and, quite obviously for whatever reason, keen to make sure I had no chance of escape. But why? What would make someone do this? I'm at a complete loss to answer these questions, and this scares me. I feel I have no control over my own life until I get the answers to these and many other questions. For now all I have is the knowledge that at least I'm not dead, and that it seems I do have one person I can rely on to help me figure it all out. What I'd not noticed was that he had taken along with him a metal flask into the cave, and now produced it for me to drink from.

"I remembered you saying about the water at the lowest point, so thought I should make the most of the chance to get a supply. Don't drink it all at once, we might be glad of some later."

"Here, do you want some," I ask, but of course he was a step ahead of me and had had his share while he was in there! He sat here alongside me while I take enough of a drink to refresh myself to keep me going wherever our journey is about to take us.

"Now, all we have to do is decide which way to go from here," and before I could even try to guess which way was South he beats me yet again by producing a compass and a map from the pocket on his rucksack.

"I reckon if we head this way till we reach one of these smaller roads we can follow it into Buxton. There's bound to be somewhere we can bunk down overnight, then see if we can hitch another lift from there down the A515."

"I did wonder," I tell him, "if we're doing the right thing to go back towards Surrey come to that. Won't the police be expecting that?"

"No chance. They'd expect you, if you were guilty, to get as far away as possible."

"I suppose you're right. But I still can't work out how I got to be right up in this part of the country in the first place. Surely I wouldn't have just found my way up here and hidden in the cave, you must be right about someone having put me there, but who would do that?" I really wish I could remember so much more.

Once again Steve is quick to reassure me that I will in time. I suppose he's right, after all there are bits of memories gradually coming back. As we plod on across the grassy hills, eventually meeting a small road signposted for Buxton, Steve encourages me to chat about myself. At first this seems like pointless waffle, but as time goes on I begin to see he has a reason for encouraging this. Though at first I struggle to know what he expects me to say, after a while without giving it much thought, I realise that some of what I'm saying begins to sound quite real. But first, by way of encouragement he talks to me about his own youth.

"I was the eldest of three boys and a girl," he tells me, "so I was always expected to be a good influence on the others, especially after my Dad died. Mum naturally assumed I'd step up and take his place."

"That must have been hard, how old were you when you lost your father? Was there much difference in age between you and the others?" I felt quite sorry for him having to suddenly be man of the house as it were.

"I was fourteen. The other two boys were twelve and ten at the time, and both a bit of a handful." At this point he stopped and seemed unwilling to go on. "What about you, did you have any brothers or sisters?"

"Yes, just my older sister Jennifer," and there it was, the answer to the mystery of who was Jenny! Without any effort too. I couldn't believe it just came to me so easily.

"Well done Mel, didn't I tell you it'll creep up on you when you least expect it? So now we know who Jenny is what can you tell me about her?"

"Well, I know she's older than me, and she's married to Alan… Alan West. I don't think I've seen her for a while, she doesn't live in Kent now."

Steve suggested a few minutes sit down under a tree along the verge. "So if she doesn't live in Kent, can you remember where she does live? Try hard to remember."

I shut my eyes tight and try to visualise her home, or something to give me a clue as to its whereabouts, and then it comes to me… I can't visualise her home because I've never actually visited her there, but I did send a Christmas card not so long ago. "She lives in a place called Halewood, not far from Liverpool, but I can't quite remember all the address."

This seems to please him no end. He opens up his map again and studies it for a while before announcing in a really upbeat way, "Yes, that's perfect!"

"What do you mean, what's perfect? Are we going to see Jenny?" I ask.

"No we're not, but the police won't know that. You see," he lays the map across our laps, "from where we are now all we need do to throw them off track is to make them believe you are going there. Perhaps we'll have a change of plan and head across to Macclesfield first. Then they'll assume you're plan is to get across from Liverpool to Ireland. Perfect!"

"So then, what will we do?" I ask.

"What we were planning in the first place… heading south towards Surrey. The last place they'll expect you to be."

As we set off on our walk he chats to me, gently prising out of my still slightly misty mind, small details to learn more about my background. I explain that, though I have lived most of my life with my parents and sister in a small village in Kent, I had gone to college in Canterbury. I then went on to do a degree in psychology at the University of London, and it was while studying there that I'd gone on a hen night with a group of girls in the city.

"Now I remember; that's where I met Jake's brother Andy."

"Ok, well done Mel, you're doing a great job," and then, seeing the way I'm struggling to dig out more from my half empty brain he says, "Don't push yourself any more though just now. As long as you've got some coming back the rest will follow eventually."

By the time we've walked for another twenty minutes we arrive in Buxton. Steve suggests that now we are in amongst more people we should split up just enough so that no one knows we're together. As he says, he can be more help to me if the police don't associate him with me. Armed with enough cash to buy a coffee and a bus ticket to Macclesfield, I sit out of the wind in the bus shelter and try hard not to look up when he does the same. He sits the far end of the shelter, making a point of ignoring me completely. It does seem strange. When the bus comes along we both climb aboard, him sitting at the front and me near the back. There are only about another six people on board as we pull out, but a handful join us along the way.

One woman chooses to join me at the back and, to my discomfort, decides to strike up a conversation. I wish she'd go and sit somewhere else, but it seems I'm stuck with her. I must try not to look uncomfortable at all, so I just smile sweetly and go along with her inane waffle!

When she asks me if I live in Macclesfield I find myself telling her that "no, I'm going on through there to visit my sister near Liverpool." I thought when I said this that perhaps I shouldn't have done, it might have been better to pretend I didn't speak English!

"You'll be going by train from there then will you?" she put to me.

"Yes, I think so," I heard myself rather feebly say. I wondered if Steve overheard, and if he did had I done the wrong thing?

Of course he had. When he got off the bus and walked away I did likewise and followed him at a discreet distance, not knowing where we were going. Eventually he vanished behind a wall, and as I got to the spot from which he'd vanished an arm came out and grabbed me. Before I could follow my instinct to scream, as when we first met, I found his hand over my mouth to quell that scream!

"I wish you'd stop doing that!" I say as soon as he loosens his grip.

"What, and have you yell at the top of your voice? You must be kidding me. Anyway, that was a good move…what you said to that old bag about heading for Liverpool I mean."

"I'm glad you approve sir," I say sarcastically. "Now what? It's getting dark. Do we find another shed to sleep in?"

"No, not this time. I think we can do better than that tonight. I saw a notice in the bus station saying something about a homeless night shelter if we can find it. Only thing is, we'd have to go in separately. I doubt they have mixed accommodation anyway, but at least it'll stop people seeing us together and be in out of the cold. With any luck they might even dish out something to eat."

"Sounds good to me," and then I hesitate. "You won't go without me in the morning will you?"

"Of course not, I know how useless you'd be on your own…and how much you're going to pay me for my services when this is all over," a comment that just for a brief second reminds me of the last time a man asked me to pay for something, but as he says this I look up at his face and can detect that (now) comforting grin.

It really didn't take too long to find the shelter as it was in a church hall. When we did Steve told me I should go in first. He said that when he came in I was to totally ignore him, treat him as a total stranger. He said I must look hard up and starving, not hard to do dressed as I am in my old torn jeans and tatty shirt, and as for starving...I am!

I'm pleased to say that the very nice lady who met me when I went in was really kind. She quickly assured me that, as Steve had suggested, no one was going to question me. She took me to a camp bed amongst a row of others and allotted me one, then took me to collect a plate of hot casserole to eat at a long table at the end of the room. Just at that minute I was so hungry I'd have eaten anything, but this meal was particularly delicious anyway.

The room was divided with screens so I had no way of knowing if Steve had actually come in until, just as I took my empty plate back, he was there collecting his meal. It was hard trying to ignore him but somehow I managed it and found my way back to my bed where someone had put a warm blanket and a pillow. I'd carried my sleeping bag in rolled up under my arm so opened it up, climbed inside, and pulled the blanket over the top.

That night I managed to shut everything bad out of my mind and slept like a log, full up, warm and comfortable.

Chapter Ten.

The next morning I woke up much refreshed, though it took me a few minutes and just a little panic to remember where I was. The first thing I wanted to do was to look to check to see that Steve was still here, but of course I couldn't see around the dividing screen. Just as I was wondering if I dare take a sneaky peep round, the same nice lady from last night appeared from a door at the end of the hall.

"You're awake at last then young lady. You certainly look better for a good night's sleep. Now, if you'd like to take this to the ladies and freshen up you can come and have some breakfast."

As she said this she handed me a blue toilet bag containing, so I found when I opened it in the Ladies, all that I needed to wash, clean my teeth, and brush my hair. By the time I came out of there I not only felt a new woman, but must certainly have looked (and even smelt!) Like one!

When I finally reappeared I was ushered to the same table where the food was dished out last night. Not that I'd need much ushering as the smell of the food being prepared would have dragged me there blindfolded. There was a dozen or more men and women, some not more than kids, passing along the line, plate in hand, grateful for such a generous offering. Near the head of the queue, as I might have guessed, and much to my relief, was the familiar figure of Steve. People were taking their plates and finding a seat wherever there was a space, and I was just lucky enough to find someone get up from their place next to him just as I'd collected my food.

He barely appeared to notice my presence, just a brief nod as if acknowledging any stranger, but when there was no one close enough to hear us he whispered quietly that he'd meet me down by the bus stop where we'd arrived last night. "I'll go first," he said, "but you take your time and follow on a bit later." Then up he got, handed in his plate, picked up the rucksack, and left.

After I'd finished eating I too returned my plate. "Thanks for that," I said with real gratitude, "and for the bed. That's the best night's sleep I've had for a while, and certainly the warmest."

"That's fine dear," said my nice lady, "anytime you need us we're always here. I hope you don't mind but I'd like you to have this to take with you," and as she said this she handed me a small rucksack. I opened it up as there was clearly something inside, and found a sweatshirt, two pairs of socks and a lovely warm grey hooded fleece. She had also put inside the wash bag I'd used earlier and a small torch!

"Are you sure you want me to have all this? Why me rather than the other girls who were here earlier?"

"Well dear, I know most of them and those who are not on drugs have homes to go to if they choose to. I don't want to offend you, but you do look a bit lost and in need of help. Now you will come back if there's anything at all we can do to help now, won't you?"

This was such a sincere act of kindness that I had all I could do not to cry, but knew if I did I'd be in danger of telling her the whole story, so I just hugged her, said a genuine thank you, and left with my new rucksack over my shoulders. What a difference a day makes?

I headed off in the direction of the place we'd left the bus yesterday but didn't get down that far before I'm met by Steve.

"Did you get a good night?" he asked, then noticing the bag on my shoulder asks where I got it from. I told him that I had had a really good night and told him how the woman there had given it to me. He quizzed me to be sure I hadn't told her anything I shouldn't, and seemed surprised as much as pleased with my answer. I gave him a quick squint at my new selection of clothes, in particular the warm fleece, and he told me he too had been given two new pairs of socks and a wash bag too, though his had a razor in it. I couldn't resist asking if that meant he would shave off his facial hair, to which he replies with a laugh, "What, and spoil my good looks!"

"So what next? Do we get back on a bus? Or do we go by train like the nosey old bag said yesterday?"

"Not likely. We need to go in a totally different direction than we were yesterday. But first we'll find a public phone somewhere so you can ring your sister. Do you know her number?" I assure him I do, "Don't say more than you have to, just that you're in trouble and are heading that way so will see her soon. Then put the phone down before she can ask anything more, do you understand?" I assured him that I did, even though I would have liked to confide in Jenny but, as he explained, this could make things harder for her in the long run.

Not having a clue just where we'd find a public phone in these days of mobiles, I said I would go back in and see if my lady from the night shelter was still there. If so she might perhaps allow me to use hers if I tell her I'm trying to contact my sister. For once Steve thinks I've got a good idea, "But don't forget what I said about short and sweet, and don't let anyone overhear you if you can help it."

When I go back I'm just in time to catch her locking up ready to go home, but when I explain that I need to contact my sister, she gives me a sympathetic smile and hands me her mobile. I can't help thinking how trusting that is of her. I could easily grab it and run. But of course I wouldn't and somehow she must have thought that too. I believe she heard what I said to a very concerned Jenny, but I followed orders and made it as brief a conversation as possible. When Jenny asked if this was to do with what she's read about Jake, I just say that I'll tell her all about it when I get there. I feel awful when she tries to tell me how Mum and Dad have rushed back from Spain (where they have a small apartment as a winter retreat) as they're so worried about me.

Even so, I reckon I managed to convince both the shelter lady and poor Jenny that I was in trouble, but both seemed comforted to know I was heading there for support.

When I give the phone back, thank its owner, and stroll off round the corner to where Steve is waiting for me I ask, "So then where are we going now, and how are we getting there?"

Though I don't know the answer to the first part of my first question I might guess what the answer to the second part would be.

"We'll head down from here towards Ashbourne, across the Peaks. It'll be a long walk, avoiding as many roads as we can, but we can take it steady. Don't worry, we'll soon get you fit," he laughs at the concerned expression on my face. He obviously sees me as a bit of a townie, and he's probably right! Though I still seem a bit vague about my past I do know I'm not the fittest person around, but I object to being made to feel incapable of a little cross country walk, and am quick to tell him so! I ask what he means by a long walk, and try hard not to look daunted when he says it's probably around thirty miles as the crow flies. Lucky crow, if only I could fly too.

So off we set, Steve stepping it out and me, once more like a kid, trudging along behind trying my hardest to keep up without looking too unfit. I must admit it wasn't too long before I could hide it no longer. "Can't we just ease up just a little?" I ask him.

"Thought you said you were fit," he said sarcastically,

"I am...Well reasonably, but if we keep going at this rate I'll be fit to drop!"

The expression on his face clearly tells me that, once again, he's having fun at my expense. Just for a few seconds I'm fuming, but then I realise that it is his easy going ways that put me at my ease with him and make me feel I can trust him, so perhaps better feeling annoyed with him than feeling in danger from him. I wonder too just how much of that way he has of winding me up also gives me the extra push I need to keep me going.

We plod on at a good pace, sticking where possible to the open countryside, away from the roads and odd villages. Just at one small hamlet Steve found me a discreet and sheltered spot behind a stone wall to rest and stay out of sight whilst he walked off, as he informed me, in search of sustenance for our walk, at a small hamlet nearby. I think I must have dropped off for a few minutes as I came to with a start with a tap on my shoulder.

"Jake, is that you..." then I realise what I've just said, and where I am. I look up at a rather surprised Steve staring down at me,

"Sorry, it's just me I'm afraid. I didn't mean to startle you."

He sits down alongside of me behind the wall and, giving me a rather anxious look, asks, "Were you dreaming about him, Jake I mean?"

"I think I must have been. I remember seeing his mop of blonde hair falling over his face. We always laugh about our matching hair … or I suppose I should say we used to. People often thought we were brother and sister. I can't believe he's gone; why would anyone do that, he's always been such a friendly, gentle person. Why…"

The reality of what's happened finally sinks in to my mind, my mind that up till now has been so hazy, almost on another planet. I can feel tears welling up from the very depths of me and I'm helpless to stop them, so I just have to let them come!

"That's it Mel, let it out. If you didn't soon give in to your feelings they'll drive you mad," I feel an arm around my shoulders and, for the second time since we met, turn my face into him and thoroughly soak his jacket with my tears! Once again, when I manage to stop the flow, I apologise but, once again, he is not bothered by it at all. Instead he hands me a napkin he'd obviously brought from a refreshment van he'd found nearby to use as a tissue, telling me to blow my nose and wipe my eyes (as if I was a kid!), then he handed me a warm sausage roll.

"I reckon it's time for you to talk to me about him, Jake I mean, and anything else you can think about to give us a lead as to just what did happen. But first tuck into that, there's another one if you need it, or we can save it for later. I couldn't bring hot drinks but I did get a bottle of milk, hope you like milk, but you can put the top back on so it keeps for a while. It keeps you going better than canned drinks anyway."

"I'm not keen but suppose you're right." I didn't want to admit it to his face but he usually was right!

"Well, I don't know if I can tell you anything very helpful. Jake is ... was, thirty-five. He was into tech stuff in a big way, that's why his business is production of new technology that I really never did understand. But anyway, he struck lucky some years back and got in on some big export deal that made a killing," I hesitated hearing myself using that word, "and that's what set him up in the sort of lifestyle he had. I'm afraid I came from a much lower type of background. Don't think that went down too well, when we got together I mean."

"So you reckon there were people who didn't approve of you being with him?"

"Well, now you put it like that I suppose there were. Jake didn't care though, if he wanted something he was used to getting it." I can't help giving a little chuckle as I add that, "I've seen grown men squirm when they tried to get the better of him."

"Anyone in particular come to mind? I guess you mean business associates?"

"Well no one in particular, he was a bit ruthless when it came to business, but he was the same with anyone who upset him, even family come to that. I believe he's upset his brother Andy more than once as he would often get annoyed with his lazy attitude to work. He'd worked hard to get what he'd got, and couldn't understand why others, including Andy, expected to get it handed to them on a plate."

Steve sat munching away at his sausage roll, obviously taking in all I have to say, yet saying very little. He's keen to know about any family Jake has, so I find myself giving him a quick run-down on all those I know.

" His brother Andy, is just a couple of years or so younger than him and is a junior partner in the business, and there's his older sister, Tracy, who is nearly three years older, but she is married and living in the States. From the way he speaks of her I think he is genuinely fond of her. He was talking of us spending our honeymoon out there so we could spend a little time with her and her family. I was really looking forward to that. I've never really been abroad, unless the Channel Islands or the Isle of Wight count!"

"Well, not really I don't think. I'd have thought he would have taken you away somewhere before now though," Steve grinned at my lack of travel experience.

"Well, not everyone gets to fly off into the blue horizon you know. How about you? I suppose you've jetted off to the Caribbean or some such exotic place?"

To my surprise, instead of some quick retort or sarcastic quip, Steve's whole expression changed. He stood up and stared into the distance, and for a few brief seconds said not a word.

When he did look round he just gave me his hand to pull me back onto my feet, and all he said on the subject was, "Yes, I've travelled, but it wasn't exotic."

There was something in his tone that once again made me decide not to question him further on the subject! I did as I was bid and walked on with him in silence.

Chapter Eleven.

By night fall, after a long tiring trudge, we still haven't reached Ashbourne. It's getting cold and almost dark when we come across a farmhouse, its lights glowing invitingly at the windows. Assuming this is where we might ask for accommodation for the night I find the energy to pick up my weary pace, but I'm somewhat surprised and disappointed when my companion steers me away from the house and across to a cow byre behind it a way.

"Surely we're not going to sleep in with the cows are we?" I ask in disbelief.

"Why not, thought you'd like a change of company," he answers with a laugh, "no, I've got a much better idea." As he says this he leads the way to the rear of the byre to where there is a hay stack with bales stacked nearly to the roof. "Right, let's see if you can climb," and points to the top of the stack.

"You don't really expect me to get up there do you? Is it safe up there for a start?" I question, probably showing concern as much due to my fear of heights as anything else.

"Put it this way, it'll be a damn site safer up there than down here if we get seen, so get climbing!"

With a great deal of help, not all given in what you'd call a particularly gentlemanly way, I find myself on top of the stack. Here I watch as Steve carefully clambers about, shifting a few bales from the middle of the top layers, leaving what looks like a nest down in the middle.

"Your room for the night miss, bit scratchy but if you wriggle into your sleeping bag I think you'll find it warm."

So there we are, eating a supper of the two remaining sausage rolls and drinking the last of the milk before settling down with our rucksacks as pillows, and wrapped up in all the clothing we have and inside our sleeping bags. After the long, exhausting trek that day I don't take long to go off to sleep at first, but during the night, probably an hour or two after we bed down, I can feel myself shivering. It seems that for all I thought I had enough on to keep me warm I was wrong. I wrap my fleece closer around me, pull the hood up and try again.

Dare I, I wonder, wriggle just that little bit closer to Steve? I can almost feel the warmth coming from him from here, but I don't want to take liberties, and certainly don't want to give him the wrong idea or put myself in any danger.

I needn't have worried as it turns out. While I was trying to decide he turned over in his sleep, and I find him up against my back, and an arm coming over me! It's obvious he is still sound asleep or I might panic, but as it is the warmth from him on my back is a blessing. As for putting myself in danger, it doesn't take much to make me realise I'm not. In fact the only thing I'm left to puzzle over as I drift off into a good night's sleep is the whisper of a name,

'Beth', muttered quietly in his sleep just once. Perhaps yet another thing I shouldn't ask about.

By the time I wake up I can see it's beginning to get light across the top of the far hills. I lay there for a minute soaking up the warmth still coming from my companion's body there behind me, until his voice brings me to with a start, "Did you sleep ok? Wish you wouldn't talk in your sleep, it's a dead giveaway if anyone had heard you." Of course I wasn't aware that I had, but then is it surprising under the circumstances? I didn't like to say I'd heard him do just that too, mumbling some girl's name. I think my curiosity must remain unanswered, for now at least.

He peeps over the edge of the stack to where the cows are contentedly chewing still. "Right, who's going down to get breakfast, you or me?" and as he says this he holds up the empty milk bottle.

"You don't mean to milk the cows do you? I wouldn't know how to do that. Anyway, they're pretty big cows at that. They might not like you doing that." As soon as I said this I knew it sounded pretty stupid, but I'd never had dealings with cows, save seeing them grazing in the fields! My comments obviously amused him no end!

"Why did I know I'd have to go," he said with a sigh, "and of course they won't mind. Anytime now the cowman will be out to milk them all anyway, that's why they're all waiting by the gate there."

"Well, just be careful then," I tell him.

"Ah, that's touching to know you care about my safety around the big, fierce cows."

"No, it's not that, I just don't want you to get caught and leave me out in the wilds on my own," I throw back at him as he starts his descent of the stack.

I watch nervously as he quietly approaches one of the cows near the gate, then, very quietly and gently, ducks down by her side, coming up a couple of minutes later holding a full bottle. I watch him climb back up, bottle in hand, but just as he rolls across to our cosy nest we hear a door slam which seems to be a signal to the cows to let go with a lowed chorus of mooing, obviously a sign that someone is coming. We duck down and keep as still as we can, not that anyone would hear us above the din below, and wait for the whole herd to be released to cross the yard for milking.

We gather up our belongings into our rucksacks and with great trepidation I climb down the far side of the stack, once again with much help. As we sneak back toward the open fields once more I can't believe the nerve of this man! Just, and only just, out of sight of the farmhouse, we pass a chicken coop, and he has the sheer audacity to open the nest box at the back and steal yet another couple of eggs! "Wrap them in something and put them in your bag until we find water," I'm told.

"Thanks for that, suppose I break them?"

"You'll have eggy clothes and you just won't get any breakfast that's all."

So off we go again, Steve leading the way at a good energetic pace, and me struggling along behind, trying not to let him see I am struggling! Luckily we'd not gone far when we came across a shallow river and are able to set ourselves up a temporary breakfast stop in a little copse nearby. I make myself useful fetching water in his can whilst Steve gets a few bits of kindling and starts a small fire to heat it. Meanwhile I decide I could wait no longer for some form of nourishment, so decide to take a sneaky swig of milk while he's busy.

"Oh yuck! It's warm," I exclaim, never having had milk directly from source as it were.

"What did you expect, a refrigerated cow? It's easy to see you really don't have much idea of country matters do you? It's perfectly safe to drink though, or failing that you'll have to get more water from the stream and drink that until the milk cools later on."

"Ok, you don't have to take such delight in making me look ignorant, we can't all have lived rough long enough to learn all the things you've obviously picked up."

"Survival tactics are a specialty of mine I must admit. No, you're right, I shouldn't make fun of you…but you have to admit you can be quite funny sometimes."

"Huh, I'm not going to stand here being insulted. I'm going down to the stream to get a drink and have a bit of a freshen up. Just you turn your back and get the breakfast cooked while I'm gone please."

"Yes ma'am, anything you say ma'am. Sorry but you can't have soldiers with it, so it'll have to be hard boiled again." As I walk away I can hear him quietly chuckling at my expense … again!

Just for once I find myself using my initiative and taking the milk bottle with me. I figure that it will cool quicker if I prop it with a couple of rocks in the edge of the river while I splash some of the drastically cold water around myself. By the time I go back to him Steve has finished cooking the eggs. Once again we sit crossed legged on the ground peeling and eating them as if they were the finest caviar, keen as we are to quench the hunger of the night. At last I also manage to gain his respect for my initiative in cooling the milk. Mind you, he won't allow me to drink as much as I really would like to have as he insists we need to keep some for later.

Before we're ready to set off again Steve tells me to stay where I am while he has a freshen up too, and a chance to check out exactly where we've got to on his map. I watch him disappear along the river bank and out of sight and can't help wondering just what he's going to come up with next. He seems to be a man full of surprises, not necessarily always good ones at that! When he does reappear I'm left speechless. Instead, as I was expecting him to do, coming strolling back through the trees, he's trudging along the river bank pulling a small rowing boat behind him!

"Come and give me a hand pulling this out," I'm told, "We can 'borrow' it for a while to ease the strain on your 'poor' little legs I reckon."

"What do you mean, 'borrow' it? Have you asked someone?" But the grin on his face tells me the answer to that one.

It seems he'd found it downstream a way caught up in some reeds. He reckons it must have broken loose from somewhere upstream where two tributaries meet making it deep enough to float this small boat, as the rope attached was pretty tatty. Come to that, so is the boat itself! It doesn't look barely watertight at all.

"So you really think I'm getting in that with you then do you? You must be joking. Why would I want to do that might I ask?"

Without looking up from the task he's taken on, he repeats how much he reckons it'll save me in energy, but then also adds, as if just in passing, that he had heard that the police had reason to widen their search to cover the Macclesfield area and surrounding countryside.

"Why didn't you say sooner, what reason do they have, and why did we stay at the shelter if you knew they'd be looking for us? You let us just walk off and then spend the night at that damn farm, and never said a word!"

"You're panicking again. Will you just concentrate on the job in hand and do as you're told women, or I'll leave you there on your own."

"Ok, so what do you want me to do then?" I consider myself duly reprimanded, but still want to know why he thinks this rickety old boat will help our cause.

We soon finish cleaning up this wreck, and it's at this point he calmly explains that the idea behind 'borrowing' this vessel is not just to save me a long walk, but to keep my scent off the surrounding land, just in case the police should bring their dogs this way to look for me! Oh my … I've never even thought of that. Why didn't he say before? That's obvious … because he knew the effect it would have on me of course.

Finding himself a good sized piece broken from a nearby tree to use as a paddle, his next move completely floored me! He got me to walk in the opposite direction from where we were heading, telling me to carry on for quite a few minutes till I come to a crossing where the water was particularly shallow. I could walk about a bit on the far side but then retrace my footsteps to the crossing and was then to stand in the water and wait.

Just as I'm wondering what this is for he comes toward me, picks me up in what I can only describe as a fireman's lift, carries me back down to the boat and dumps me in it!

"What the hell was all that performance for then?" I threw at him, "You do realise that my shoes are now soaking wet I suppose? Was that really necessary?"

"You really have no idea about these thing, have you? Well, let me explain. If the dogs do come, they will follow your scent the way you walked, but hopefully lose it where you lost contact with the ground. Oh, and by the way, my shoes are soaked too!"

"Couldn't I have taken them off first, or you too come to that?"

"You could have done but your feet would have got cut to pieces on the stony bottom. Don't worry, they'll dry out quickly enough. At least you know your feet have been washed!"

As I sit watching him push us off from the bank in our beautiful vessel, I look up at him and am torn between laughing at him or pushing him overboard. I choose to do neither in the end, just sit back against our rucksacks and enjoy the ride.

He has to use his branch to guide us carefully away from the edges to prevent getting caught on reed and shallows as we go, but it seems it works well in the same way one would be used to direct a punt. I just hope Steve can balance well enough stand up in here without falling overboard, after all, he does look rather tall standing in such a small boat. I know there's no way I could keep my balance, so it would be more than my shoes getting wet if it was down to me.

We've gone some way and the river was now building into a much more substantial one as we travel along its length. In fact it has now begun to rock our poor little vessel quite violently as the current builds. Overhead there are black clouds heading toward us fast. I gather from what little he's told me, that Steve had hoped to continue rather closer to Ashbourne than we are now, but he has now decided that it would be far safer to get onto dry land before the threatening storm breaks. Consequently, he pushes us in to the river bank and helps me out. I assume he will either tie the boat up or just let it float off, but I'm wrong on both counts … again.

Just as the rain begins to come our way, he gets me helping to haul it up the bank to where there is a small clump of trees. Then he instructs me on how to tip it upside down, prop it up on a log each end, and turn it into a small but dry, temporary shelter, just big enough for the two of us and our bags!

Here we sit for what seems like an age, and I for one am starving. When eventually the rain passes over we gather everything up ready to move off. As has happened on the occasions when we've not actually been where there are 'facilities' to use, I just have to tell Steve I need a minutes privacy. He's quick to get my drift, and says that I should go through the trees behind us while he intends to break up the remains of the boat. As he says, if anyone finds it they'll assume it's been wrecked on its passage down from where it started.

I've only gone a few yards from where we've been taking shelter when I come to what must be a derelict cottage. Can it really be empty? I'll sneak up and check it out.

After walking cautiously around it, peering in at the cobwebbed windows, I tentatively try the door latch. It opens with a creak but easily enough. I'd guess it's not been used for many years, going by the cobwebs hanging like paper chains across the corners. It seems it doesn't have quite the facilities I've come in search of, but outside there's the remains of an old fashioned 'hole in the ground' one! Oh well, any port in a storm, as the saying goes!

A minute later, just as I'm heading back to Steve, the rain begins to spit again and the sky begins to get darker again. I make a dash back to where he's still breaking up the boat, and tell of my find.

"Right," he tells me, "gather up an armful of this and we can make bit of a fire to dry out our shoes."

So saying we pick up our belongings and an armful of the driest pieces of wood we can, throwing the rest in the river, then make a dash for the shelter of the cottage.

I must admit to feeling a bit let down at this point. Having laid our sleeping bags down to sit on, and eventually climb into, set out our shoes neatly in front of the little fire place in which we've carefully laid our firewood, I was extremely disappointed with Steve! Knowing how ingenious he's always been, I was waiting to see him rub two sticks together to light it … instead he got a cigarette lighter from his rucksack and lit it with that!

Chapter Twelve.

Being under cover, and having had just a small fire to keep us warm and dry our soggy shoes to a wearable level, we drank our small remaining amount of milk, but no eggs today!

Even so, by the time we were packed up he soon had us back on our route march, or so it seemed to be, and it wasn't so very long before we found ourselves in the historic town of Ashbourne with its many timber framed buildings, and a wonderful four sided Millennium Clock in the centre. We found a bakers shop with tables and chairs outside and Steve told me to sit there and he'd get us a coffee and two packs of sandwiches while he enquired about transport to Birmingham.

What a treat to sit on a chair and actually have a coffee, even if I was told under no circumstances to eat all the sandwiches, "We'll need them later," adding firmly, "And don't speak to anyone while I'm gone." Then off he went leaving me sitting there alone, feeling rather lost and trying not to look too conspicuous.

A fairly short time after he'd left me, but just as I was beginning to get a little jittery in case he'd decided to go and leave me sitting here, he came strolling back up the road toward me in his usual casual manner.

"Don't look so worried," he said seeing my expression, "did you think I'd gone without you?"

"Wouldn't put that passed you, I'm sure you could find something better to do than babysit me," I say.

"Not likely, I'm a glutton for punishment. Besides, as I said before, you'd never cope on your own now, would you."

As before, that remark brought a sharp and rather unladylike answer from me. Anyway, he has decided that we need to go to Birmingham. He says that that being a big, busy place, it'll be easier to stay hidden in the crowds while we decide on our next move. Apparently he says that to do this we need to spend most of our remaining money to go by bus, first to Derby, then on the National Express to Birmingham.

"So then what do we do for cash?" I ask.

"Use our initiative," I'm told, leaving me none the wiser but having to accept that answer as it's the only one I get!

Within the hour we're on the way to Derby. Whatever else I don't know, I do know as soon as we arrive there that this is not anywhere I've been before. We have a while to wait for the National Express to arrive so pass the time having a wander round to keep warm. There's quite a sharp wind blowing. We make our way toward the cathedral hoping to seek shelter there. Steve enquires at the door if there's any cost to enter and is told no, but it seems we can't go in anyway as we can't take our rucksacks in. The steward at the door tells us that they only allow small bags for security reasons, which is understandable but disappointing.

He suggests coming back another day but we explain we're just passing through, but thanks anyway. I for one must look particularly cold and desperate for shelter as we turned away to go in search of another place. No doubt it's for this reason that before we've gone more than a few yards from him that the steward calls us back,

"If you would really like to come in and look around you can leave your luggage with me for a while. I have an office here and I'll keep them safe for you if it helps."

We are pleased to take up his offer, and duly thank him. I'm sure he has taken pity on what he assumes are a couple of down and outs, but even so this is not only out of the wind but an amazing place to see. We hand over our luggage, I can't help thinking a little grudgingly on Steve's part, and as we wander away he comes after us and hands us a voucher for a couple of hot drinks from the café, saying they were surplus from some earlier coach trip. Do we believe him? Do we care? We just thank him and go in search of the café to redeem them.

We stay for nearly an hour, by which time we have had our drinks, made use of the toilet facilities, and wondered at the sheer beauty of the building. By now it's time to go and catch the National Express to Birmingham, so we collect our bags, thank our kind host, and head back out ready to battle against the wind.

I'm a bit worried about us having to spend so much on the fare, but it seems there's no option. According to the timetable it should only take around an hour and a half maximum, possibly less, but then we're in no particular rush I suppose.

On the journey I can't help noticing an old lady in the seat opposite keep glancing across at us with a very disapproving expression, or is it that she recognises me from somewhere, newspapers or tv? I nudge Steve and whisper my concerns in his ear, but he whispers back that she's more likely thinking what a scruffy pair we are. The next time she looks our way, just to stop her being so nosey, he throws her a smile and says,

"Sorry we're a bit of a mess. We've just been on a hiking honeymoon you see, haven't we darling?"

I'm speechless! I certainly wasn't prepared for that one, but then I never know what to expect next from him. I try to replace the look of annoyance I was throwing his way with an equally sickly smile as the one he's showing me at that moment, "Yes dear," I reply, hoping she doesn't detect the sarcasm in my voice.

Anyway, it worked. From then on every time I looked her way I got a look which said how lucky I was, and what a lovely couple we make! Huh!!

Before long we reached our destination and disembarked, glad to walk away from our new admirer. I try hard to smile at her as we pass by, but only very briefly so that she has no chance to way lay us as we go.

"Now what, where do we go from here," I ask, "and what do we do for money?"

"Don't you worry about that, there's always ways and means of earning that, and as for where to go, there's bound to be hostels and the like where we can bunk down for a few days, all we need to do is find one."

The coach had arrived at Digbeth in Birmingham, and on enquiry it seemed that close to the bus station there is a convenient backpacker's hostel. We made our way there to see what chance there was of a cheap bed for the night and just how much it would cost. The chap at the desk appeared oblivious to our rather tatty appearance as he informed us that there was one space left, a bunk bed for two in a mixed dormitory of six beds. Though I'm a bit dubious of sharing a dorm with mixed sex companions, Steve is quick to jump in and say that we'd be happy to take it. "My sister won't mind sharing, she's not shy," he says, once more earning a look of sheer incredulity from me, which would have been something far more physical if the manager hadn't been watching at the time.

We are told about the facilities, best of all as far as I'm concerned being the laundry. It will be good to get a good freshen up of both us and our clothes. Although breakfast is included in the cost, it seems we are allowed to use the kitchen to cook any other meals for ourselves. All we have to do now is find a way to earn money to buy food and to keep our beds for more than the two nights we have enough for now. We are given a complimentary cup of coffee to welcome us and shown to our dorm.

After we find ourselves sitting side by side on the bottom bunk gratefully sipping our drinks, we discuss tactics. Perhaps I should say that Steve outlines what he sees as the tactics. He says that if I want to go and do our laundry then, whilst it's washing, come back and make the most of the chance to rest, he will go out and see what he can find by way of fund raising. I must admit that on this occasion I'm glad to do as he suggests.

A while later, having been along to transfer the washing from the machine to the dryer, I went back to the dorm and must have dropped off propped up against the pillows on the bottom bunk as I woke up with a start by a sudden noise then a voice.

"Well hello there young lady, what's your name?" said the figure looking down on me. I was about to say Mel, then I stopped myself, just as the door flew open and a more familiar voice answered for me, " This is my sister Annie, not that it's any of your business, so keep away from her mate."

The figure asking my name backed away in haste assuring us he was just trying to be friendly as we were sharing the dorm. We went and collected our clothes from the dryer and as soon as we got back to the room I was told in no uncertain terms to move my stuff up to the top bunk. I must admit to feeling a little easier to find that two of the other occupants of the room were also women, though I tried not to get too deep in conversation for fear of saying something I shouldn't, and I have to say that it was warmer on the top bunk.

Before turning in for the night we went for a bit of a walk around the immediate vicinity. Steve pointed out a pub as we strolled around tucking into a very welcome feast of burger and chips.

"I've asked around for casual work and the landlord there is desperate for bar staff. Have you ever worked behind a bar?"

"Not that I know of. I think I'd remember if I'd done that," and then, with what must be a look of horror on my face, "You haven't told him I have? And even if I had, wouldn't I be a bit exposed there?"

"Don't panic, I was joking. I told him I can do that…you've got a job in the kitchen doing the dirty glasses! It's ok though, all you have to do is put them in a dishwasher and take them out."

"That's ok then. You had me worried for a minute."

"It doesn't take much to do that now does it?" he laughed.

He tells me we start tomorrow lunch time, giving us chance to get into the swing of it before the evening rush. It seems he's quite happy to take us on as casual help which means no questions asked or official details given. How Steve swung this I've no idea, but if it means we can have accommodation and eat for a few days I for one am happy to go along with it.

"I suppose bar work is yet another one of your many talents then is it? Been used to a cushy life behind the bar have you?" I throw at him.

"I wish. Perhaps that's what I should have done." Then, after a short period of reflection, "but I've done a bit of it, and spent more than enough time the other side of the bar to know how it works."

By the time we'd finished our burgers we were back at the hostel. I was more than glad to clamber up to my bunk and snuggle into my sleeping bag for a much needed night's sleep, safe in the knowledge that I had Steve there below me to ward off any unwanted interference.

Chapter Thirteen.

We had been together for a week before our arrival at Birmingham, but it feels as if I've known Steve for years. Of course we have been rather thrown together through circumstances, mine rather than his of course. Actually, to be truthful, I have no idea just what his circumstances are; he won't open up to me, and I wouldn't presume to ask. He's never ever touched on the subject of why he chooses to live the way he does, but he's obviously done it for long enough to feel perfectly at ease with this way of life. I've no idea why he chooses to take me under his wing but I must admit he is right, on my own I wouldn't have a clue how to cope with my situation. I know, or at least I think I do, that he was only joking the time he mentioned me paying him when this nightmare was all over, but right now I'd gladly give him everything I have … assuming I do actually have anything to give!

So far our time in Birmingham seems to be the most relaxed we've had. Steve seems different when he's behind the bar at the pub, somehow easier going with others, yet still quite guarded in his own way. He'll laugh and chat to the customers, yet I notice the same reluctance to talk about himself as I've seen since we met. I can't help feeling there is so much about him that he keeps locked away from everyone, me included, yet it's so deep in him that it's more than I dare to do to push him for anything he chooses to keep to himself for fear of the reaction I might get. At this stage I am just glad to have his guidance and protection to help sort my problems, and hope that perhaps he will eventually feel he can open up to me.

But still, his personality alone brings its own rewards in the form of tips which, added to our wages, means that we soon manage to accumulate a good stash of funds for our expedition... wherever this takes us!

Other than popping into the bar now and again I prefer to stay hidden in the background as much as possible. Steve is such a big personality when he's in a good mood that no one gives me a second glance. A week on from our first shift I've managed to get my hair coloured and cut properly which certainly makes me feel a lot more human. I've also been allowed to buy myself a couple of sets of new under clothes and new tops, though he warned me not to get anything that would stand out too much. I don't mind that, just as long as I can get rid of those old grotty things I'd been wearing when I escaped from that awful cave, but for whatever reason he still insists I should stick them down in the bottom of my bag and hang onto them for now!

Though I'm keen to head off in search of the truth about Jake, part of me is terrified about what we might be getting into. Part of me just wants to bury my head in the proverbial sand and start a new life here as Annie, Steve's sister. Most of the time I am living in this imaginary existence, and just pretending the world comes to an end outside Birmingham! He was quite right in as much as it is so easy to become just another nameless face amongst so many in a busy place like this.

During the day when we're not working at the pub, we spend our time looking around the many galleries and museums Birmingham has to offer. On a couple of really good, spring like days we bought a few things to make up a picnic, and went to Calthorpe Park. The spring flowers were shooting up all around in the beds, geese were laying lazily by the side of the river, and the occasional group of joggers were often passing by. On one of these days we made ourselves comfortable under a large chestnut tree and watched the world go by as we ate our food.

"That's what we should be doing to get you fit," Steve joked as the joggers go by, or at least I hope it was a joke.

"I'm not so unfit I know, anyway, how come you're so tough? Surely living rough doesn't necessarily make you that tough, does it?"

There I go again! Saying the wrong thing. I can see by the look I'm getting that my casual comment, only meant as a joke though it was, once more brings an instant flash of…of what? Temper, regret, a memory; who knows? I certainly don't, but I just wish he felt he could talk to me or that I dare to ask.

Anyway, I quickly change the subject by suggesting we feed our crusts to the geese. We have been sitting on his sleeping bag, Steve never wanting to leave belongings in the hostel during the daytime unless we are there with them, so while I go to do this he puts his sleeping bag back into his rucksack. I can't help laughing to myself at the way he is almost stuck to his as if it holds the crown jewels inside! Perhaps it does, maybe I should have had a good rummage back in that shed while I had chance to.

As we wander back through the town ready to do our shift at the pub, there's a young chap, I reckon about eighteen, sitting in a doorway of an empty shop. It's obvious that he's homeless, and certainly not having much luck with the busking he's tried with the guitar by his side as he seems to have given up trying.

I'm quite taken by surprise when Steve stops and asks how long he's been living rough.

"About a month I suppose," came a rather sullen answer.

The boy just sat starring at the ground, not really looking inclined to communicate at all.

Steve stood looking down at him briefly before saying, "You're obviously not happy with it. Why not cut your losses and go home?"

The lad threw a quick glance at Steve which clearly said 'what would you know about it?'

"I bet I've been living rough a lot longer than you lad. Now, just how did you get to be doing it at your age? You're not on drugs or anything are you?"

"No, of course not! Just got no choice that's all. Anyway, I can't go home, I ain't got one. "

"What do you mean by that? Why haven't you got one?" Steve asked.

"I got put in care when I was six, passed from one foster home to another till I got kicked out at eighteen. They found me a job in a factory and digs in a cheap hostel for a couple of months, but the firm went bust, so no job, no hostel. So here I am, getting nowhere!"

"Well, there's enough folks about here, I can't see why you're not having more luck playing this?" Steve picked up the guitar and strummed it a couple of times.

"Probably because, I'm not much good. I can sing but my playing ain't much cop. So it ain't getting me anywhere."

To my surprise Steve puts down his rucksack, puts the strap over his head, and strikes up with a rendition of 'Stand by Me', straight away attracting the attention of those passing by, and encouraged to do so, the lad gets up from the doorway and joins in, singing as if they'd been rehearsing for months! It's a treat to watch and listen to them. I take the initiative and put the guitar case opened up in front of them, and before too long contributions are coming from all sides. I can't help thinking they make a good act together.

About an hour and a couple of cans of coke later I begin to wonder how he'll ever fit the guitar back in its case for the money in there! When they do decide to stop, the lad who's name at this point we've not bothered to ask, looks a different person to the deflated and bedraggled one we'd come across earlier. He now has a broad smile across his face.

"Why did you do that?" he asks Steve.

"Someone had to get you off your arse and make you believe in yourself. Now pick up that cash, put your guitar away, and let's get something to eat. I'm starving."

Josh is more than happy to suggest treating us to something to eat, but Steve says no, he's got a better idea. So now he has two of us trotting along with him like a couple of strays! Though we're still quite early for our shift at the pub, we get there just as the lunchtime meals are being finished and the early staff are clearing tables. Steve wastes no time in suggesting to the landlord and the chef that it's a great shame to see good food go to waste, and that there are three of us who would willingly help dispose of any unwanted helpings!

"What you mean is, you're on the scrounge I suppose? And who is this stray you've picked up might I ask?" he asks.

Neither of us having thought to ask, we both look to him to answer this one.

"I'm Josh," he explains, "I hope you don't mind, but Steve and Annie said to come with them?"

The landlord told him to go and fetch a plate of something from the kitchen, then turned to us to ask where we found him. Steve explained Josh's story, also rubbing in what a hard time he was having trying to survive living on the streets, "and through no fault of his own. I doubt he'll survive out there for long before someone gets him hooked on drugs or something!"

Talk about laying it on with a trowel, he sure can tell a story I'm thinking. Anyway, it worked. By the time we've joined him in the kitchen Josh is tucking into a helping of steak and kidney pie and mash. "Suppose you two want some too?" asked the chef. Well, we were hardly going to let it go to waste after all.

While I finish mine Steve gets up and goes through to the bar. When he comes back the landlord is with him.

"Steve says you could do with work, is that right lad?" Josh looks up from his plate and says that he does need to find a way to earn something to live on.

"Ok, tell you what, I'll give you a month's trial run. Don't suppose you've worked behind a bar before, but you're never too young to learn. You'll have to be prepared to do Annie's job collecting and washing glasses too sometimes, is that ok?"

"Do you mean that man? Yes thanks, that'll be great. Are you really sure about this?"

"I'm prepared to give it a go if Steve says you're worth a try. Besides, I'm going to be shorthanded when these two leave."

I throw a look of bewilderment at Steve, I knew nothing about us leaving. He throws me one that says not to question it right now. I guess it's because we've been here for some time and he said from the start we mustn't stay anywhere long enough to get recognised.

Then, turning to the boss he adds the information that young Josh has a good singing voice and can play his guitar 'reasonably well', so would come in handy if they had a karaoke evening anytime. "How about having one next week to see how he gets on? Reckon you'll be pleased with him."

"Ok, you don't need to rub it in. I get the picture…you want me to keep an eye on him?" Then turning to the lad, "Do you have anywhere to stay?" to which the answer was of course negative. "Right, there's a small box room upstairs. Needs a bit of a clean-up, but if you're prepared to do that and it's big enough, you can use that while you're working here. I'll have to do paperwork and make it all official mind, employing someone your age you see."

"That's brilliant, thanks. I don't need much room and I promise I won't let you down."

For the rest of the evening Josh spent some time cleaning and tidying up the room which is now going to be his home. The look on his face said everything, words were not needed.

As we said goodbye to him that night it was all I could do not to shed a few tears…but I know I'd be laughed at if I had!

Chapter Fourteen.

We spend another week staying at the hostel and working at the pub. It seems that there has been mention on the tv and in the papers about 'Melanie Cook' having been sighted by an hgv driver who reported giving a girl answering her description a lift to the outskirts of Chesterfield, though he said she was calling herself Jenny. This led the police to believe this was possibly the person they were looking for as it appeared she has a sister by that name. There's no mention of me having Steve with me so this must have been that horrible man who picked me up first, not Norman in the van, as he would have mentioned Steve.

I feel in such a turmoil of emotions. The time we've spent here has had the effect of calming me and giving me chance to recover from what's gone on. It's given me chance to bring back things my mind had blocked out, though still leaving me mystified as to what happened to my poor Jake. No matter how hard I try to think back, I'm certain he was still alive when I last saw him, yet even though I know he sometimes wasn't the easiest man to get on with, I'm sure he wasn't bad enough to drive anyone to murder. Steve did suggest me making a list of those I reckon could be considered candidates for the crime, but none I've listed were really particularly likely choices. In fact I feel pretty guilty adding most to the list. Most were people he'd dealt with to do with business over the last few years, but I don't think any of them would have gone to such lengths. After all, they were business men, not criminals or ruffians.

Of course I didn't really get too involved with his business. I knew Andy and a chap called Tony Brooks were partners in the firm, and I knew the names of a couple of his associates that I heard him talk about once or twice. There were two I remember him saying had left at one time. It seemed they had fallen out with him and chosen to leave the company. I don't think they were too happy when Jake refused to pay them redundancy money, saying that he'd not made them redundant, they left of their own free will. Even so surely they wouldn't go to the length of murdering him. The thought made me shudder.

"So where do we go next," I ask Steve, "Is the next journey down to Surrey?" Though I can't say I really want to go back there I assume that is where we're aiming for eventually. To my surprise the answer to this question is no.

"We will eventually but there's somewhere else I need to go on the way. All I've got to do is find transport to get there."

Obviously I ask where he has in mind, but find him surprisingly tight-lipped on the subject. In fact I feel almost as if this is something personal to him, and that I mustn't even question him further on our destination.

I think we will both be sorry to leave our little safe haven here, especially the pub. I really wasn't ready to go back to the life out there, living on the streets as before. With young Josh there I feel I've come out of hiding in the kitchen so much. Though he spent time helping me with glass collecting, filling and emptying the dishwasher and helping the chef, Steve has also taken him under his wing, teaching him the basics of bar work. On the last evening we are there we get an unexpected surprise. The boss has obviously been encouraging him to be more outgoing, and between them they have arranged a karaoke night.

It is so good to see how much at home he now is, and to hear him entertain with such confidence. Even his guitar playing seems to have come on in leaps and bounds since we first met that day. Before too long, as I knew would happen, he handed the guitar to Steve and they performed once more as they had before. This time I find myself brave enough, along with the rest of the punters, to sing along. Whatever else has happened or will happen in my life I doubt I have ever been, or will ever be as relaxed and happy as I feel this evening. Of course, they finish of, as I knew they would, with a last rendition of 'Stand by Me', the song that had brought them together, and brought Josh to the chance of a new and better life. As I listen to this I can't help thinking just how appropriate the words to this last song are to me; Right now, as it says, 'I won't be afraid, as long as (Steve) stands by me'.

110

Saying a final farewell to everyone there, especially Josh, is so hard. He put down the last of the glasses from the bar as I come into the kitchen with Steve, comes over to me and gives me a huge hug. He turns to Steve, who is quick to say, "Don't even think of giving me a hug like that!" Even so, the grin on his face is enough to show the lad it's worth a try. With a 'pretend' look of disgust on his face, Steve accepts one anyway then, talking to him like a sergeant major, tells him in no uncertain terms to keep up the good work, don't let the boss down now he's given him this chance to make good, and,

"Stop saying you ain't much cop any more. Have faith in yourself or no one else will. You can be who you like if you put your mind to it lad."

As we trudge back to the hostel late that night we are both rather quiet. I want to ask once more where we're going and how we'll get there, but I'm still aware this is a subject I shouldn't ask questions about until I'm told. At least we won't be without funds this time after saving up much of our earnings while we've been working, plus the sizable extra bonus the boss gave us for getting him out of trouble when he was shorthanded.

"Do you know how good that was of you to get young Josh taken on there? He's so happy now, a changed boy. How did you know they'd have him there?"

"I didn't, but I knew they'd be shorthanded when we left, and he needed someone to keep him out of trouble…like you do!" He pulled a face at me as he said that, "Seems I'm good at picking up waifs and strays."

"I beg your pardon. I'm not a waif or a stray thank you,"

"But you do need someone to keep you out of trouble though don't you?"

Once again he's right, but I won't tell him that even though he is. I really don't know what to make of this man sometimes. He seems a strange mixture of different characters, sometimes he's like my best friend or big brother, strong, clever and reliable. Yet there are also those occasions when I find him more like a stranger, distant and extremely scary, almost dangerous! Even so, whichever character he's displaying, I'm so glad he's decided to help me.

Back at the hostel that night we sorted our belongings into our rucksacks so that all we'd need to do the next morning was add our wash things and sleeping bags. At least all our spare clothes were now clean though, but I wonder how long before we get another chance to do any washing, and I must say I feel so much better for having had a period of not being such a tramp!

"Don't get too used to it though, there could well be a time when we'll need to fade into our old rough look to disappear again," I'm told.

We pay our dues for our final night, thank the hostel manager, and head of out into the chilly morning air with our rucksacks on our backs. I turn to Steve as we set off along the road and ask what the plan as regards transport is, quite expecting the answer to be that we use our feet, but instead of this I actually get a vaguely acceptable, though not particularly positive one.

"I don't know yet, but don't worry, it's too far to walk this time. I'm still trying to figure it out. Don't worry though, we'll get there somehow."

I know he didn't really want to tell me why we are going to wherever we're heading, but at least it would be nice to have some idea roughly in which direction this is. Oh well, I suppose I'll just have to do as I've done all along and wait to see where I'm led! I am beginning to accept this now after all.

It soon becomes apparent that we're heading back to the coach station which we'd arrived at what seems like an age ago. That looks promising, perhaps he's as good as his word, and we're not doing another route march this time! I stand by and wait while Steve goes to collect tickets. It doesn't immediately register in my mind just how trusting I'm being, standing obediently waiting for him to buy tickets to go God knows where, and not thinking to question him…or is it that either I don't care, or don't dare? I think right now I'm past caring as I can't see any other solution to my predicament than to just leave it to him and go with the flow.

It's not long before he comes back armed with tickets and hands me mine. I'm still none the wiser as to our destination or reasons for going wherever it is. Oh well, he's obviously got something in mind.

"Should we do as we did before and sit apart?"

"No, not this time. I've just picked up a paper to read and seen something new on the inside page. I'll show you when we get going, but let's try to get a back seat. Stop looking worried, you don't want to attract attention now do you?"

He's right again of course. Why can't I keep my fear under control, appear unconcerned like him. I'd like to ask him how he manages to do that but feel it's probably one of those questions he'd think would just prove how hopeless I am, so I won't give him the satisfaction!

We have a bit of a wait for the bus as we seem to have missed an earlier one, but at least we have time for a coffee. Rather than show me the newspaper article when we're on the bus Steve decides he might as well show me now. It's headed 'New information on missing girl'. Keep cool girl I tell myself, determined not to let him see the panic I'm feeling inside. Of course I'm not fooling myself, and certainly not him.

"I know what you're thinking but you need to read carefully and see just what new information they do have. It's not as bad as you're thinking."

I duly take a deep breath and study the article, which I have to say is not particularly big anyway, but was just confirming what Steve had told me before, though in a little more detail. It seems that someone had reported sitting on that bus to Macclesfield chatting to a young woman, but though she thought this young woman looked similar to the police photo of Melanie Cook, she had short dark hair, not long blonde hair as they had described her. When questioned by the police this woman told them that the girl she'd spoken to was alone, and was heading for Liverpool to visit her sister.

"Oh hell, I wish I'd never spoken to the nosey old bat now. Now they know I've dyed my hair."

"Yes, but they also are even more sure you're heading for Jenny and Liverpool. And another thing, they still think you're on your own," Steve was quick to reassure me, "and we're going in exactly the opposite direction and you're not alone now are you?"

"It's ok for you to say, I don't even know where the hell we are going. I wish you'd not be so 'cloak and dagger' about these things, can't see what's so wrong with me knowing where you're taking me and why."

"If it puts your mind at rest, we're heading across to East Anglia. As for why, that's a private matter, so don't bother asking again. Here comes the bus. Now this time we need to look like a couple who've been together for some time, got it?"

Obediently I nod my agreement, take hold of his hand (just to make it look convincing!), and walk to the bus. We're lucky enough to get the seat at the back where Steve surprises me by putting an arm round my shoulders and whispering in my ear to put my head down and pretend to go to sleep. "That way your face won't be quite so obvious." It hadn't occurred to me that there are cameras on board buses these days until he points them out. Of course I'm glad to oblige, anything to stay out of the limelight, and besides it feels good to cuddle up to him. I had a disturbed night last night, partly because we were leaving this place we've felt so safe in for what seems like an age, but partly because I woke up in a cold sweat once, dreaming of my Jake lying cold and dead by my side in our bed! I haven't mentioned this to Steve, I don't know why, but I'm just happy to feel an arm round me in the hope of it forming a wall to shut out such thoughts. Before we've gone very far on our journey I'm out to the world until he wakes me saying we have to change to another bus.

I find we have arrived at Milton Keynes at another quite busy bus station. It turns out there is quite a wait for this connection but I'm happy to stretch my legs and move around for a bit so we go for a short stroll about, no doubt with the idea of livening me up, before going into the cafe for a plate of pasta and a drink before climbing on board the next one. The problem with this of course is that by the time we get going again I'm wide awake and so find it hard to 'act' sleepy, keeping my head down again, when I would really like to look out the window at the scenery. I have to content myself with nothing more than a sneaky glance over the bottom of the window once in a while.

"Are we going to Cambridge," I ask having seen the destination on the front of the bus.

"No, well not exactly. We're just passing through it. Why, do you know it?" He asks.

"A bit. I've been there a couple of times with Jake when he came on business. It was summer, and we sat on a wall near Kings College Chapel eating ice cream and listening to a busker. The ice cream was good, but not so sure about the poor chap busking, even though he did get a large group of foreign visitors gathered round listening to him! I have to admit you and Josh sounded a lot better." I couldn't help a little inward smile to myself over the memory of it.

"Sorry, no time for sightseeing today so just put your head down and keep quiet," so I do as I'm told and say no more.

Chapter Fifteen.

It seems from the odd sign I manage to spot that we are heading towards Bedford first where we stop to pick up more passengers, but then we do carry on in the direction of Cambridge. Though I have been to Cambridge in the past it was a while ago now and I can't say that I would remember my way around, and I certainly don't have a clue about anywhere else in the area to give me an idea as to our final destination, so I will just sit back and enjoy the ride as best I can. I must say I'll be so glad when we do finally arrive at Cambridge, having to travel all this way in this position is getting pretty uncomfortable now.

On arrival there I knew from somewhere down in my memory, that there was a designated bus station, Drummer Street I think I remember it's called, but to my surprise, not to say horror, these coaches don't pull in there but go on past this and actually pull up almost outside the police headquarters further round the corner.

"Oh hell," I say, "do you think anyone will see us?"

"Only if you get off looking so bloody guilty, so pull yourself together," I'm told in no uncertain terms.

Now where too I wonder? All I can do is tag along and see where I'm being taken. I'm not altogether sure that I like being left in the dark like this, but the alternative is to be on my own, and I certainly don't like that as a plan either! Not much of a choice really is there?

We walk back along the road to the main bus station and I stand there like a spare part while Steve walks up and down surveying the assorted boards, presumably to determine which bus to get to take us to wherever he wants to go. There are three buses in right now and one has started its engine ready to leave when he suddenly turns and beckons for me to get there quick as it was about to go. I dash over as quickly as possible and climb aboard, taking a seat while he pays the fares before joining me, still not knowing our destination as I'd not been quick enough to look before getting on board.

In just a little over an hour I see a magnificent tower looming up in the distance. Steve at last condescends to tell me that this is the tower of Ely Cathedral which, he adds, is known as the 'ship of the fens'. I have to admit that this is all new to me. I know I've certainly not been here before as I know I'd have remembered that. By this time it is around four o'clock and I for one am glad to get off the bus and use my legs before they become completely seized up. We do seem to have spent an awful long time sitting in coaches and buses today, though I suppose I can't have it both ways after complaining about the long treks he's been taking me on.

I rather assumed, wrongly as it turns out, that now we've reached here I would get to find out why we'd come, but not so. What Steve does do is to walk me round past the outside of the very imposing cathedral, promising that we would go inside sometime, perhaps tomorrow, but just not

119

today. Then he points me in the direction of a house which it seems once belonged to Oliver Cromwell. He then gives me enough money from our fast dwindling supply to visit this, and suggests that I should then go further down the road to the museum which he reckons will keep me busy for some time. When I ask why he isn't coming with me he tells me he has a private matter to attend to, and that I mustn't question him about it.

"I'll meet you back where we got off the bus when I'm finished, but just do as I ask and don't follow me, do you understand?" These last words were thrown at me with such a force that I felt almost threatened. His attitude had changed in the distance of a few words, yet scary as they were I can't help feeling curious. After all, what could he be up to that would be so bad? Still, I said I did understand, and that I would go to look at the places he'd suggested, and meet up later.

Yet, as I watch him marching off away from me and disappearing out of sight, curiosity gets the upper hand. I've got to see what he's up to after all, haven't I? It seems he knows the area, perhaps he's got a girlfriend or something here. Perhaps he's visiting Beth? After all he did speak her name in his sleep once. Perhaps she dumped him and he wants her back? Or perhaps he just knows somewhere to steal something useful and reckons I'd be a burden? Whatever it is he obviously doesn't want me to know about it.

I make up my mind almost as soon as he's out of sight, I'm going to follow him…at a safe distance of course. I pocket the money he's given me and set off, though at the pace he's walking I'm having a job keeping up with him, and of course this is made worse by having to stay out of sight. At first it's not really so difficult as he goes off round some of the smaller roads with corners I can hide round. Eventually this becomes more difficult when he hits a bigger road with less cover for me. I find I need to hang back some way and worry I could lose track of him. At one point he crosses onto another road near enough as open as the last, so that I still worry about losing him, even losing myself come to that. Why am I doing this I wonder? I'd stop and go back but now I've come this far I feel committed to my quest!

Expecting that he is either meeting or visiting someone, I am taken completely by surprise seeing him cross into a lane which runs off to the right of this road, follow it a way, then disappear from my view. From where I am there seems to be no sign of any houses, just a row of very tall fir trees. It's not until I get to the same spot that I realise that the place he's gone is actually a large cemetery!

I certainly wasn't expecting that. Now what, I wonder? I creep into the entrance and am pleased to find a good covering of trees and shrubs to hide amongst. I do wonder if I should retreat fast and give him the privacy he wanted. Yet I am still curious. He hasn't struck me as the sort to go visiting graves from what I've seen up till now, he's far too hard and down to earth for that. Perhaps he's meeting someone here? Or perhaps he buried hidden treasure here at some point and is coming back to dig it up? Once more my mind is going into overdrive thinking of the possibilities, most of which are verging on the ridiculous.

I edge as close as I can without being seen, in some ways wishing I'd gone to the museum as I was told, yet knowing that my mind was not going to allow me to rest until I'd solved the mystery of just what he was up to here.

Well, he doesn't look as if he's meeting anyone anyway as there's no one else here. I can see him a way off just standing looking down at two of the graves. Then, to my absolute astonishment, he gets down on his knees and runs his finger round the letters carved on each of them. I'm pretty sure he's talking quietly and that, even from this distance, I can see tears running down his cheeks. This can't be the big, tough Steve I've come to know. Perhaps I don't know him as well as I think I do. He's certainly a man of mystery in so many ways, but this seems totally out of character.

I find myself feeling quite embarrassed just watching from my hiding place here behind this tree, but I daren't move for fear of being caught, so I have to just stay put and be patient. I feel so guilty, as if I'm intruding on something I wasn't meant to see, but I'm here now and must just stay out of sight and never let on that I've been here. After all, though he said to meet him back where we'd got off the bus, I was under the impression that he intended us to stay around Ely area somewhere at least for tonight, possibly for a few days. That being the case he wouldn't be surprised if I said I decided to do the museum tomorrow. I might get away with telling him it was a bit busy so I just went for a walk around the town or something. Seeing him right now I doubt he'll care too much what I did anyway.

He must have sat down there between two stones for a good half an hour, clearing the overlapping grass from around both whilst talking quietly and gently. I can feel my heart going out to him in what is obviously a moment of some distress for him but I know I'm helpless to do anything so can only stay hidden until he chooses to leave.

Eventually he gets to his feet, taps the top of both stones, mutters something gentle and quiet, and walks away wiping his eyes on his sleeve as he goes. I've not seen him looking so pathetic since we met! My heart tells me to rush over to him and throw my arms round him, but my mind tells me this would be an unwanted intrusion of his privacy, so all I can do is keep quiet and keep out of sight until he's gone.

Once he's gone I must admit I'm glad to move. I've been standing rigidly still for so long so as to stay hidden away that my legs feel for a minute as if they don't belong to me. I have to stamp up and down a couple of times to get the circulation going in them. Now I know I should follow him back up to the town, but it's not going to be easy staying hidden again. The good thing is that it's now beginning to turn quite dusk, actually verging on dark, so with luck that should help me to stay under cover. I'll just give him a head start before making my way back.

Now I know I've made plenty of mistakes since I started this journey, but the one I make now has to be the worst one so far! I don't know why I have to be so stupid sometimes, but this goes well beyond stupidity.

I just can't leave this place without being nosey, my curiosity just takes over my common sense, and I creep forward toward the two gravestones where Steve had been just now. I peer at them to read the inscriptions but it's too dark. Then I remember the little torch the lady at the night shelter in Macclesfield had given me. I take my rucksack off and rummage about until I find it then, after putting my bag back on, I switch it on and look down.

The first one reads,

> Here Lies Claire Lockett, age 32.
> Beloved daughter and sister
> Always in our hearts.

Oh my God, this must be Steve's sister. He said he had one but never told me her name, or that she had passed away. I turn my attention to the other stone and stare in disbelief at this which reads,

> Here Lies Elizabeth Lockett, age 30
> Beloved wife of Steven
> Also Sean, age 2 years.
> Loved forever.

Looking at these inscriptions I suddenly realise with a shudder of sheer horror running through my whole being that the dates on both stones are identical. Both read, 18th October, 2016. Whatever caused this to happen to his sister, wife and son all at the same time? Oh my God, what a nightmare this would have been.

There's a crack of a twig behind me, I drop my torch into my pocket, but before I can move I'm grabbed forcefully from behind and spun round to face a furious Steve. Before I have chance to speak I'm shaken hard, slapped across the face, and flung to the ground with such force I thought I'd broken my ribs. He pulls me back up and shakes me again, this time shouting at me at the same time,

"You interfering, stupid little fool. Why couldn't you do as you were told, JUST FOR ONCE; what gives you the right to poke your nose into my business. Go on then, have a closer look," and as he said this he practically threw me down on the ground so hard I hit my head on one of the stones.

I try to say something, to apologise, but he's in no mood to listen to anything I might say. I go to get up but he pushes me back down and holds me face down with his foot on my neck. Oh my God, I'm going to die, he's going to kill me. I've got no defence against the onslaught of pure hate that's coming from this man, I now see just what he is capable of and it absolutely terrifies me!

He moves his foot from my neck and bends over…I really think this is the end for me, but then he grabs me roughly and quite literally throws me off the stone I've been on and falls down on his knees beside it.

"Get out of here, now, go."

I can see a mix of hate and sheer wretchedness in his face as I crawl away to a safe distance. Twenty minutes ago I would have been happy to comfort him, now I'm just too scared to be anywhere near this man. All I can do now is to scramble to my feet and take off as fast as my extremely shaky legs will carry me. The last audible words I can hear as I go are "I'm sorry, so sorry." I've no idea if this is aimed at me, I'm not going to hang around to find out, but after the way he turned on me, could it be meant for his family who all seem to have died together? Did he lose it and turn on them on that day? Did he kill them? He's clearly more than capable of it, but surely not.

I've no idea where to go or what to do. Of course, under normal circumstances if I'd been attacked like that, I would automatically go straight to the police and report it, but these are not normal circumstances. Yet I know I must get away from here fast. I just don't think I can trust him anymore. I'm shaking from head to toe and I don't think I've ever been so scared in my life; even though I still can't swear my memory is as good as it should be yet, I'd surely never forget such violence .

Not having been here before I really don't know where to go, so I decide to make a dash for the place we'd arrived on the bus earlier. Perhaps, if there's one still going, I could head back to Cambridge. I think I have a little knowledge of the place, though not perhaps as much as I wish I had. All I have to do is find my way back, hope there's a bus going that way still tonight and, more importantly, be sure to watch out for Steve. I've no idea if he is following me or not, but if he is I dread to think what he'll do if he catches up with me. The very thought makes me shudder!

Now the light has nearly gone it's difficult finding my way back to look for a bus, even more difficult trying to peer into the dim shadows to watch for my attacker. Feeling as battered and bruised as I do I must look a right mess, so I'm happy to stay out of sight as much as possible. When I get to the bus stop I keep back in the shadows, watching all the time in the direction I've come from and praying the bus will come before he does. Perhaps he won't, perhaps he's just happy to be rid of me, especially after this, but if he did what would he do?

I'm on the verge of giving up on the chance of a bus when one comes along. Realising at the last minute I only have the money I should have spent at seeing the things I should have visited, I fish around in my pocket and manage to find just enough to cover the fare, even though I get some annoyed looks from the driver for taking so long fishing it out while he's waiting to go.

Sitting in the bus looking out I can't help wondering if Steve is out there looking for me, perhaps even seeing me being driven away, out of his reach.

Why did I do it? Until then I had someone to keep me safe, show me what to do. Now what have I got… Nothing!

127

Chapter Sixteen.

By the time the bus pulls into Drummer Street it is pretty dark and chilly, and what's even worse is that I have about ten pence to my name. How I'll find anywhere to spend the night is beyond me, especially after the day I've just experienced.

So here I am, cold, hungry, homeless and penniless, a situation I know Steve would have had a solution to. He always did. But he's not here, and after today he never will be again, and I only have myself to blame for that.

Now I have to stand on my own two feet, but I really feel so very lost on my own. With not more than a few pence left, not enough to buy food even though I'm starving, I'm feeling absolutely on my knees. The last meal I've had was the dish of pasta we had at Milton Keynes, but that was hours ago. Serves me right, I should have spent it on food at Ely if I didn't want to go sightseeing, instead of doing just what I'd been told not to do, then having to spend it on running away from the one person I wish I could be with right now.

As for where to sleep tonight, I've absolutely no idea. I wonder if I'll end up in a shop doorway. Oh well, it serves me right. At least I have a sleeping bag and a few bare necessities now, and a little more idea of how to survive out here than I would have had before I met Steve. I suppose I'll have to learn to deal with such things on my own now anyway. On the other hand I remember that the bus station where I'm standing right now is only a stone's throw from where we'd got off the National Express earlier that day, almost outside the police headquarters! Should I call it a day and hand myself in, perhaps even confess to Jake's murder and have done with all this hastle. After all, Steve was right when he said I would never cope on my own, and that's how I am now through my own stupidity.

It's soon clear to me that there's no way I'd be allowed to bed down in the bus station itself, so I wander off in search of a sheltered place, probably a doorway or the like, prepared to wrap up in all the clothes I can get on from my rucksack, then wriggle into my sleeping bag. Unfortunately it soon becomes clear that the only ones there are already have occupants, not particularly pleasant ones at that. When I do find what looks like an empty sleeping bag and try to push it over with my foot to make a space, I'm bombarded with a stream of abuse from inside it! It sounds very much like someone well drugged up, and I really don't want to get into that sort of thing again after my earlier encounter, so I slink off before he decides to poke his head out to see me.

After a good hour just wandering about with no luck I give in! I'm going to the police to throw myself on their mercy. At least I'll get a warm, dry cell, and perhaps a bite to eat. The final deciding factor comes on my way there.

I'm passing a pizza take away on route and the smell really hooks me. I fumble in my pocket to see just how much I do have left, but only find the ten pence left from my bus fare. I can't help it, I have to try so I go in and approach the counter.

"Yes young lady, what can I get you," asks the chap behind the counter.

"Well you see, I'm in a predicament," I looked at him to see his reaction but he was waiting to hear what I had to say before reacting, "You see, I've lost track of my partner and he's got all our money with him," Now I could see his face react in a way that said 'pull the other one'. I smiled my best desperate smile and pushed on, "I find all I've got in my pocket is ten pence. Could you please give me ten pence worth of pizza to keep me going till he gets here, please?"

Without hesitation or emotion he stares me in the face and says, "No, but I'll give you my toe up your back-side if you don't get out of my shop right now."

This really is the final straw. I really have no choice but to head to the police station to hand myself in, I just can't carry on any more like this. I walk off across the green space between the shops and the police station feeling thoroughly defeated. Just before I cross the road to go into the building I sit for a while on a seat I find here and find myself reliving the day's events.

It had all started so well. Steve and I had been relaxed and happy leaving Birmingham after our pleasant week or so there, our befriending of Josh and the leaving party they'd thrown us. Even the long draw out coach journey had been pretty relaxed and comfortable, and as far as I was concerned worry free, that was until we reached Ely.

From then on everything has been sheer disaster, all of my making. I had hopes of proving my innocence in the matter of poor Jake's murder, but only with Steve's help. I messed that up… and for what? Just for the sake of my stupid curiosity. Now here I sit in the dark on a park bench, with no food inside me and nowhere to sleep out of the cold night air, and my only solution is to walk across the road and get myself arrested for murder, murder of a man I loved dearly. I sit here, head in hands, crying bitterly, knowing that this is the only solution, but desperately wishing I could turn the clock back, at least to this afternoon if not to before the murder.

I must look a pretty pathetic mess sitting here as a couple of minutes into my bout of self-pity I feel a tap on the shoulder and a voice saying hello. I look up, half expecting it to be one of the local constabulary from across the road, but I'm wrong in that assumption. It's another woman, I guess a few years younger than me. She too has a rucksack on her back and looks a bit scruffy looking, but seems pleasant enough from what I can see through my tears.

"Are you ok? I saw you in town a while ago. Are you looking for the shelter?" She threw questions at me without giving me chance to answer, except for the last one, the one that caught my attention as soon as it left her mouth.

"Shelter, do you mean there's a homeless shelter here?"

"Yes, of course there is. It's not far from here, just a little walk round the corner there. That's where I'm going now if you want to come. I know they've got room for more. The foods pretty good too if you're hungry, and the beds are clean. I'm Sally by the way."

I smiled gratefully at her for the information and, even more so, for the offer of a friendly smile just when I needed it most,

"Thanks Sally, it's just what I do need and I appreciate you bothering with me. I'm sorry about the fuss I was making but I've had a hell of a day. My name's Annie,"

I thought after I'd said it that perhaps I should have thought of a new name, just in case he came after me! What a thought, would I be pleased to see him or downright terrified? I decided to take what might be a safe option by adding that, "but I'm usually called by my second name, Pat. Not many people call me Annie thank goodness."

I hoped I'd convinced her enough to forget the name Annie as much as possible.

"Ok Pat, let's go and find you a bed for the night. Are you staying more than one? I thought perhaps you were like a lot of us, students with no accommodation. There's all sorts stay here you know."

"No, not really. I'd quite like to study here, supposing of course I'm not too old, but right now I'm just in a bit of a spot as regards money, and no one to turn to that I can trust. Bit of a long story, but I'd rather not talk about it if you don't mind."

She didn't, thank goodness, so we walked on a short distance up the street to the shelter she had said about. It was a relief to find she'd been right in saying they had plenty of room for me right now. It seems that during term time some students find themselves without accommodation and have to resort to shelters such as this one, but right now they are still on their Easter break. Well, that's the first and only good thing that's happened to me all day... or at least since we got to Ely earlier.

I was in time to get a plate of hot casserole just before the kitchen lady went off duty for the night, and then I was told to go with my new friend Sally, who had introduced me as Pat to the staff. There was a spare bed in the small room she slept in. I must say it was so much better than I'd hoped for. It was clean, warm and comfortable, and went a long way to healing my wounds, well at least the psychological ones anyway, on a temporary basis anyway.

It isn't until I get undressed for bed that poor Sally gasps in horror. "Whatever has happened to you? Have you been attacked? You're covered in bruises. Who did this to you Pat? You should report this to the police you know. Do you want me to come with you?"

"It's not so bad really. No, I wasn't attacked, I fell down the steps off the bus that's all. I just bruise easily. It'll disappear quite quickly, you'll see. I can hardly go to the police and say I was too clumsy getting off the bus now can I?" And though I try to laugh it off as a bit of a joke I doubt for one minute she believes a word of it, any more than I can convince myself I'm not in any pain from my wounds. I'm just glad to be alive, even if not to tell the tale! Even so I am shocked myself when I get a look at myself in the mirror in the ladies toilets. I've got a dirty great bruise on my forehead, just as the last one has disappeared too, but the worst one is across the back of my neck and shoulders, which is where he pinned me down with his foot. But I'm certainly not about to tell anyone that as I still feel guilty for pushing him to it.

As I lay there after the light goes out I think back over the terrible events of the day. Still the predominant thoughts in my head take me back to Ely and those two graves. As much as I know I should at the very least hate Steve for the way he attacked me, how can I when I could see the grief he was suffering from his awful loss. Sister, wife and baby son, all dying together; I've absolutely no idea how, but however it happened it's clear he's suffering drastically. Then, just to make it even worse, I have to ignore his wish to grieve alone and stick my nose in where it's not wanted just to feed my curiosity.

Can I really blame him for his reaction when I brought it on myself, or was this the real Steve? Is he really capable of, not just attacking me, but even being responsible for the deaths of his family? I don't know what I should believe any more.

That night, tired as I am, all I can do is lie here torn between such a drastic mix of emotions that I don't think I slept for more than the odd half hour here and there and when I do I invariably wake up in a sweat, dreaming of anything from being in that cave, to seeing Jake dead, and then a vision of Steve's face filled with such rage staring down at me.

Thankfully Sally is a heavy sleeper and doesn't hear a thing. In the end I give up trying to sleep and settle for just resting, yet even being awake doesn't really do much to stop the same thoughts going round and round in my head. Morning will be a blessing.

Chapter Seventeen.

Back at Ely, immediately following the terrible outpouring of grief and rage combined, Steve could do nothing more than crouch down, huddled up and just allow his tears to pour out freely, more freely than he'd ever allowed himself to do since that terrible day, the 18th October 2016. Up until now he'd always ignored those who told him he needed to open up and talk about it, face it head on as it were, and find a way to deal with what had happened. He had always refused to listen to what he called the 'do gooders', and deal with what he saw as his own problem in his own way, and his way was to push it away and try to forget it.

But of course, when it comes to it, forgetting such a terrible thing is just not an option. Pushed into a dark corner of the mind as this was, such things have a way of festering and causing irreparable damage to any sensible thought processes. Sooner or later something or someone would force it back up to the surface, and the longer it has been buried, the worse the effect it will have.

For Steve this time had come, and the someone forcing it to the surface just happened to be poor Mel. Perhaps, he thought, he should never have allowed her to get close enough to him to do this. Perhaps he should have stayed a free spirit, roaming alone forever. But something had brought her into his solitary existence in need of help, and he had felt it wrong to just ignore this need in the same way he'd ignored his own need for help for so long. He supposed it was the feeling of them sharing their lost identities and both, in their own ways, needing help to work out their different problems. Or perhaps it had something to do with both having lost their soul mate? Maybe it had something to do with a deep felt feeling of guilt they both carried in their hearts over these loses?

Whatever the reasons that had brought them together, up until tonight these reasons had had a therapeutic effect on both. Up until tonight Steve had found that perhaps he could still play a useful part in the world. As for Mel, he liked to think he was giving her the support and protection he'd not given to poor Beth, and certainly not to his son Sean, nor even his dear sister Claire, but now he knew he had let her down as well. He was left feeling completely wretched, probably more so than ever before.

She'd gone, where to he had no idea, but even if he did she'd certainly never trust him again after the way he'd treated her tonight. He wished he could turn the clock back to the time when she did trust him, but it was too late, she'd gone off to get away from him and he had no way of knowing where to. Why did he do it?

The thought that by being alone she could put herself in danger after his efforts to protect her since they met, weighed heavy on his mind, but then not nearly as heavily as the danger she'd been in from being with him tonight.

He knew now, now that he'd pulled himself together, that it was time to stop his self-pity and act. He must find Mel, he must try, not to make excuses, but to explain why he'd acted the way he had, and hope she would accept his apology. Not for his sake but for the sake of her own safety, he had to try, he had to hope. But where should he look, where would she go? He knew she'd never been to Ely before, and by this time most places were closed. There were the pubs. Perhaps she would have gone in one of them to ask for help, but then of course she knew that there was the chance that the locals might know him, so she'd be reluctant to take the chance of them telling him she was there.

No, that's not a likely solution, but what was? Would she chose to sleep rough; after all, they had done this quite a few nights since they first met. Even so, where would she go to do that? All he could do was roam around the city, looking in all the places he thought might be possible. There were doorways but he knows she'd be aware he'd be looking for her, so that was unlikely. He walked down along the river hunting for a sheltered place she may have found, but with no success at all. He was quite pleased in a way as the obvious place in that direction would have been beneath the bridge on the towpath. He knew of old that this area was usually occupied by all the dubious characters from the district, mostly those high on drugs, and she'd learnt to avoid them back at Chesterfield! He made his way back up toward the cathedral hoping, though he knew it was locked up, that she may have taken shelter in the porch, but this hope too drew a blank.

The thought crossed his mind that she may have jumped on a bus, but the last one had gone some time ago and, even if she had, where would she have got off? If he could be sure of this he would willingly walk all night to find her, but where to walk too eluded him right now, and even if he should know where to find her would she want to be found, could he ever gain her trust again after the way he'd treated her earlier?

By this time Steve was feeling sheer panic invading his mind. He'd not allowed anyone or anything to drive him to this state for over two years now. He thought he had taken full control of any remaining emotions that threatened to take control of him, but this had just been an illusion. He could see now that all he'd been doing was suppressing them rather than controlling them. Since meeting Mel he had thought it was him helping her to overcome her fears, but now he could see that perhaps it was her who was helping him overcome his. He knew now he couldn't turn his back on things anymore, he must face them head on, but he also knew that to do this he must first find Mel and beg her to forgive him. He must help her find her way out of the mire she'd found herself in before he could climb out of his own.

He decided that the most likely possibility would be for her to have jumped on that last bus back to Cambridge. After all, he did remember her mentioning briefly about visiting there with Jake once. He could wait for the early morning bus, but he knew he'd never sleep if he stayed there, so he put his rucksack on his back and set off along the road he knew would eventually get him there. Finding her when he arrived would be a difficult thing to do, assuming she was actually in Cambridge, but that was a problem he'd face when the morning came.

By the time morning did actually arrive Steve was in Cambridge and wondering where and how to go about trying to find Mel. He'd tried wandering round when he arrived during the night but other than the assortment of rough sleepers curled up in sleeping bags, some with their dogs curled up with them, there seemed no sign of her or anyone who had seen her. Truth be told, none of them had any interest in her whereabouts nor did they appreciate Steve's disturbance of their night's sleep. In the end he had to admit defeat and await daylight before resuming his search.

He had realised early on that she had little or no money on her and was worried as to how she would go about getting food and shelter with none. Another problem he realised he had was that he had no idea what name she was going by. They had called her Annie whilst in Birmingham, but she could well have changed that to avoid him finding her. He'd trained her well, he thought, and knew she was picking up just how to stay hidden. Perhaps he shouldn't have taken so much trouble to teach her!

Not being familiar with Cambridge, Steve had to spend a couple of days getting to know many of those rough sleepers he came across. He was determined to persevere in his search for Mel but to do this he knew he had to win their trust before they would even consider bothering with this stranger asking so many questions. He got them to point him in the direction of the different shelters and food banks, hoping he would come across Mel at one, but he knew he had to be extremely careful as she may well either have reported him for assault, or at the very least be taking steps to avoid him. It was no hardship for him having to integrate himself into the rougher elements of Cambridge society. He'd walked out on so called 'civilised society' long since, at a time he'd felt he had no real place in it. Up until now he'd had no reason to want to change that, no real purpose worth bothering with. Yet until that awful incident in Ely, though he hadn't been aware of it, he just needed something to pull him back to reality rather than hide away from it. In Mel he'd found that something, but now he'd lost her and with her his new found sense of purpose.

He knew he must find her, and quickly. The hunt for Jake's killer was still well toward the front of most of the national newspapers, and it was clear that, due to her disappearance, Mel was top of the list of suspects. He'd even read one report that mentioned another possible sighting outside Macclesfield, heading across the Peaks. He'd been right to consider the possibility of a search with dogs, but it said that this had been inconclusive! Though they had moved on well since then, and were now well out of that area, he knew that complacency would be fatal.

All he could hope was that she would keep out of sight, yet that would of course prevent him finding her, and he knew she would be in a terrible mess right now, both mentally and physically.

For the best part of the week Steve kept up his desperate search, all the time feeling deep remorse for his actions and trying everything he could, even using the story of how he was looking for his younger sister, Annie, who had left home following a row! But for all his efforts he was to reap no reward.

Chapter Eighteen.

The first morning at the shelter I found I had eventually managed to drop off into some sort of sleep, but even that was filled with unsettling dreams, the sort which leave you feeling more tired than if you'd stayed awake. I awoke with a start, being disturbed by someone upstairs banging a door shut. To me it sounded like gunfire, though not having been close to gunfire, I have no idea why I should think that, it was just the first thing that came into my head. The nearest thing to that sound I'd heard was the noise of that explosion in the cave.

For some reason I can't help thinking back to that awful morning when I came too in the complete darkness of that cave, and I am reminded of those three questions I'd had haunting my mind then… Where am I? Why am I here? Who am I?

To an extent these three questions are almost as relevant now as they were back then. Looking around me, just briefly I cannot recognise this place immediately, but after a short moment of panic I remember that this is the shelter in Cambridge that my new friend Sally brought me to last night.

As for the question of why I'm here, that's so much more involved to answer. There is certainly more than one answer to this. To answer this I needed to go over and over the events of yesterday, back to the journey from

Birmingham to Cambridge, from here on to Ely, and from our arrival to that otherwise beautiful old city when I for one was feeling relaxed and safe. It was from that point on that things were to turn against me, leaving the only option open to me to take off into the night and find myself back as I started, alone, lost and scared!

Once again this took my mind reeling in recriminations, partly aimed at myself for refusing to respect Steve's wishes when he asked to be allowed a little privacy, but partly aimed at him for his drastic overreaction to my stupidity. Though I know I am very much to blame for my lack of discretion, at the same time I wonder, was it really necessary for him to act quite so violently?

Still the question of 'Who am I' hangs around my mind. I know I'm Melanie Cook, but does this make me the murderer the police are looking for? I know I'm not Jenny. Jenny is my older sister, probably the one who by now is frantic with worry as to where I am, especially since I rang her to say I was on my way to see her.

Then of course I have also been known as Annie, Steve's sister! That was the best nom de plume so far. There was something comforting about having him as my 'big brother'. But now even that offers no comfort at all, and I find myself morphing into a new person called Pat. Where that name came from I have no idea, just a spur of the moment, rabbit out of a hat moment as it were!

So here I am, waking up in a place I don't know, for reasons I'm still not sure of, and assuming a name that I've fished out of the ether. Now what?

"Oh good, you're awake then are you? You're just in time for breakfast. I could tell you had a pretty restless night, so I thought I'd leave you to wake up in your own time," Sally said with a kind smile on her face. "You've just got time to freshen up first then I'll wait for you and introduce you around. It's never easy being a stranger in a new place is it?"

A part of me is really grateful to her for the friendship she's offering, but there is a part of me that would just like to be left alone to lick my wounds, figuratively speaking. As for my real wounds, I would really just prefer to keep them covered up, though of course Sally has already seen them last night.

It's not until I go to have a wash that I see just how much blacker the bruising looks this morning. I wash as fast as I can so that I can cover up again before Sally or anyone else can see what a state I'm in, but just as I think I'm nearly finished, a new face appears behind me.

"Ouch! That looks bad. Where did you get that awful bruise on your neck?" asks a voice from behind me.

I spin round, pulling my jumper on quickly to cover it up, but of course it's too late. This stranger has already seen the worst one.

"Oh, um, hi. I'm Pat," I say in a rather feeble tone of voice, "I had a bit of a tumble getting off a bus yesterday, and I reckon the bruising has really come out this morning."

"You should sue the bus company for damages," said my new companion, "I'm Vicki by the way."

"Pleased to meet you Vicki, have you been here long?" I don't know why I asked that, it sounded a bit formal but I suppose it was the first thing I could think of to take the conversation away from my bruises.

"Only a couple of weeks. Just came to check out student accommodation before term starts. The place I was at was pretty crap. Are you here for the same reason? Where do you come from? I mean, what part of the country?"

I can't help wanting to tell her to butt out, mind her own business, but as I don't know how long I'll be here I suppose I'd better not be rude. Before she has chance to pry any deeper into my affairs, along comes Sally to take me up for breakfast. I don't know what it is about this Vicki that I find so aggravating, but I could tell straight away she was the sort of person who would pick at you like a kid picking a scab, until she gets right to the bottom of what doesn't concern her.

Anyway I'm pleased to find that Sally manages to put herself between Vicki and myself at the table. This makes it harder for her to dig any deeper into my business. I think she takes umbrage at this because it's not long before she says a brusk goodbye leaving just the two of us at the table for a few minutes while we finish our drinks.

Sally threw me a rather worried look. "Are you sure you're alright? You know those bruises do look pretty horrific. If you don't mind me saying, I don't believe for one minute your story about falling off a bus. If you had the driver would have seen you got proper attention."

"I expect he would have but I didn't wait around to give him chance," I say, but I know I don't even convince myself, let alone her.

"Ok, far be it for me to poke my nose in to your business, but it's just that the last time I saw bruising like that it was closer to home as it were. My step-father used to come home drunk most nights and turn on my mum. One night I was there when he started on her, so I tried to stop him. Of course then he turned on me, and I thought he was going to kill me." She winced at the memory of what had happened,

"If it hadn't been for the neighbour calling the police I'm sure he would have."

"What happened to him, and what about your poor mum? Is he in prison now?" I ask her.

"Yes, he is now, but they won't keep him forever like they should. Poor mum has been moved to a safe house in another area for her own safety. So that's why I'm here, where he won't find me either."

Poor Sally, what a terrible ordeal to go through? Now I can see just why she's so worried about me. I'd like to be able to assure her that my bruises were not caused by being beaten up by a man… but can I really do so without lying?

147

How can I explain that I brought these on myself, not the result of some drunken bully, without sounding as if I'm making excuses for the man who did this? I'm still in a quandary myself as to how I feel about what happened, how Steve had acted.

Part of me would love to confide in her, to have someone to share my burden with, but then I would have to risk telling her the whole story. Where I'd met Steve and why I was there in the first place. About the police looking for me as a suspect in Jake's murder, about how Steve had helped me keep safe, keep out of sight all this time, how I'd always felt I could trust him totally right from the start.

There just is no correlation between this and the story of him beating me up. If Sally truly believed it had been him who did this to me she would certainly not believe, not for one minute, that I'd ever felt as safe with him as I know I did.

Without pushing me further Sally gets up from the table and I follow her to hand in our plates. She asks as we leave the room what I'm doing today, but to be honest, I have no idea. "I think the first thing I need to do is go on a hunt for a job of some sort. I've only got about ten pence to my name! Don't suppose you've got any suggestions where it's worth trying?"

"What sort of work can you do? Shame you haven't got a student card, some places take them on without too much question. Otherwise you could try on the market, or the pubs get a bit busy this time of year. They often need extra help."

"Yes, I have done a bit of pub work in the past, I think I could cope with that. I just need to get a bit of money behind me right now, then I can find proper digs, not that everyone here isn't very helpful, but I'm just not sure what I want to do just now. To be honest with you, if you hadn't come to my rescue last night I'd have been starving hungry and sleeping out in the cold or asking to be tucked up in a nice police cell for the night!" Little did she know this was as much a possibility as a joke. "Thanks for your help though Sally, it means a lot to me."

"Well I could hardly walk by and ignore you sitting there looking so bedraggled. Such a sorry sight you were!" Sally laughed as she said this, but it was clear from her tone that she was also more than a little concerned for me. "Come on then, I'll show you where to go. Do you know Cambridge at all?"

"Only bits of it. I did come here once with…," I hesitated. I was about to say Jake, but realised in time that this was risking it a bit. If she'd followed the news she might put two and two together sooner or later, "with a friend."

"That wouldn't by any chance be the same 'friend' who gave you those bruises I suppose?" I could see by her expression that she really wasn't expecting me to admit to this, even if it had been true. Anyway, it wasn't Jake; he would never have done this to me, so I had no scruples in

149

giving an honest answer, and carrying on denying her suspicions.

She didn't push it further but just said that, if I should decide to change my mind about getting the police involved, she would always be happy to come with me for support. Let's face it, that's the last thing I wanted to do after all!

True to her word Sally takes me round to meet the publican from a place not far from the market square. It seems he knows her pretty well as she does the odd shift there when he gets busy and, as luck would have it, he is going through a really busy time right now.

"Have you had any experience at waitressing?" he asks.

I'm quick to assure him I have and, being a trusting person as she is, Sally backs me up. Bearing in mind we only met last night I reckon that really is so trusting of her.

"We tend to get crowds of foreign visitors this time of year while the students are not about. Don't suppose you can speak foreign languages can you?"

"Well, I think I know a bit of French, but not fluently." As I say this I realise that this is something I didn't remember being able to do since my memory loss. It seems he's not impressed by that, even if it does mean something to me.

I'm taken on for a few shifts, some of which I get to work alongside Sally. The work is hard, sometimes verging on frantic, but it's giving me chance to put a few pounds in my pocket and begin to feel relatively safe, at least for a while. Of course I still don't know the long-term answers to the questions floating around in my mind. I really wish I knew what I should do next? Can I just be Pat and stay here forever or will I be found out? Another worry constantly on my mind is the one I find most concerning; where is Steve, is he looking for me, and what will happen if he finds me?

Part of me wishes he would find me, to be here to help and guide me as he had done since we met; yet part of me lives in dread at the thought of just what would happen if he did find me. Would he still mean me harm, or would I be safe? Even thinking about it sends a shiver down my spine! Perhaps I should give serious thought to what to do and where to go next.

Chapter Nineteen.

By the end of the first week of him being in Cambridge Steve had walked in and out, up and down every nook and cranny in an effort to find Mel. Never having been in the city before this had proved quite a feat. None the less he was determined not to give up unless he was convinced she wasn't there any longer. He had known that this was where she'd gone on that terrible night when she'd been so scared of him that she'd had to take off alone, but he had no way of knowing if she was still here or had moved on and, if she had, where would she have gone?

In his usual resourceful way he had found no difficulty in managing to survive himself, but he knew Mel was not truly capable of going it alone. He hoped that, wherever she was, she was being helped but also staying safe. Safe! What a word he thought for him to dare to use after the way he'd treated her. If he had not given her cause to take off like that he knew he could have kept her out of danger.

Cautiously he'd strolled about getting to know many of the street folk he found who regularly sat in doorways or hung around busking for a few coins, often to fund their addictions or buy the next drink. Of these he would ask, as casually as he could manage, if any had seen or heard mention of a girl by the name of Annie. If anyone bothered to ask why, which very few did, he stuck to the story of the sister who left home following a row. Even for all his efforts, Steve's search drew a complete blank. He began to think that it was useless, that she'd moved on, but where to? That was his concern. He desperately needed to know she was safe.

Now and again he would stroll casually into the odd pub, ostensibly for the purpose of buying a meal, but in the knowledge that Mel had spent that period in Birmingham getting to grips with waitressing and the odd bit of bar work, so there was always the possibility she might turn to it again to support herself. He would order either a drink, or if he could afford it, a meal, and sit discreetly at a table in a quiet corner, just nonchalantly watching the staff passing in and out of the kitchen. He rarely asked them about 'Annie' for fear of appearing a stalker.

All this time he earnt a few pounds working an odd shift or two at a hand carwash to fund his meals if nothing else, but was happy to carry on sleeping rough, often hidden from view in some park or other rather than in the heart of the city. After some days, and just as he was considering trying his luck at other towns around the area, one rainy day he dashed into a pub he'd been to before to get out of a particularly heavy downpour. He ordered a steak pie and a pint and sat, as he'd done previously, at a quiet table in the corner where he could look out of the window to check out passers-by ... just in case she walked by!

When his meal came to him it was delivered by a girl he'd not seen on his last visit. Worth a try he thought, never hurts to try chatting up a pretty (well, prettyish) girl anyway! You never know what information she might have, possibly about Mel with any luck.

"Hello, I don't think I saw you last time I was in here did I?"

"No, possibly not. I only work odd shifts. You're not a regular here either are you? Do you live in the area or are you just here on one of the sightseeing tours?" she asked.

Throwing her what he hoped was his best winning smile he told her, "not really, though it's quite a place isn't it? No, the main reason I'm here is to find my sister. She had a row with her boyfriend a few weeks back and ran off. Everyone's worried about her."

Without giving it much thought Sally, for that's who this was, as she wiped down the table looked up at him and asked, "What's her name, your sister I mean?"

"Her name is Annie. She's about your height, short dark hair, and often wears a blue beanie. Any chance you've seen her at all? I'm really worried about her."

Immediately Sally heard the name Annie she stopped what she was doing and took a fresh look at this 'friendly' stranger. She remembered Pat had said her name was actually Annie but was known as Pat. Could she be this chap's sister? Or could his tale of being worried about her be a ploy to trap her.

After all, if her friend Pat was one and the same as his Annie, is it possible that he might have been responsible for the terrible bruises she'd seen and the frightened state of mind when she'd first met her. In spite of what Pat had said she had thought right from the start that someone had caused both the mental and physical damage, and this man looked well able to do both if he had a mind to. Sally's mind was racing. What should she do? How could she find out the answer to her questions without arousing his suspicions? After all, Pat was still maintaining that she'd not been attacked, that her injuries were just down to an accident, but this certainly didn't ring true with Sally after the experiences she had suffered herself in the past.

"It's still pouring out there, not fit for ducks," she said with a light hearted laugh, "Can I get you another drink while you wait for it to ease off?"

"Oh go on then, why not, I don't fancy drowning out there when I can stay dry and have good company in here. What's your name anyway? Mine's Steve by the way."

"Good to meet you Steve, I'm Sally." Now what to do she wondered? How could she find the truth of just who this is and if it is Pat he's looking for? She had no idea. What worried her most right now was the knowledge that he might come back later that day when Pat was actually on shift! Perhaps she could find a way to persuade Pat not to work that day. Perhaps it would be best to tell Pat about this man calling himself Steve. She wondered if that was his correct name, and if so would Pat recognise it?

Unfortunately the opportunity to put her friend off her shift proved impossible. She had hoped to find her back at the shelter getting ready, in which case she'd decided to suggest they skived and treated themselves to a visit to the cinema together. As it turned out this didn't work out as Pat wasn't there when Sally got back to the shelter. Apparently she had gone off an hour sooner to call at a shop for some new socks and the market for some fruit on her way as she was partial to an apple to eat for her break during shift.

Little did Sally know that as 'Pat' was at one end of the market buying a couple of apples, Steve was approaching from the other direction in his never ending, yet apparently casual, search for his 'sister'. Without realising it the pair passed within no more than three stalls length of one another, but there just happened to be quite a crowd of foreign visitors blocking the space between, making it impossible to spot one another.

Sally had by this time decided to volunteer for an extra shift at the pub. This was the only way she could think of to keep an eye on Pat. Of course she had no way of knowing if this Steve chap would come back, but at least if he did she'd be there to see Pat's reaction, and call for help if it was needed. She'd checked him out and already decided she would be no match for him if the need arose, but there were plenty of male bar and kitchen staff to call on should the need arise. Though he'd seemed friendly enough to her earlier, in fact she'd thought him rather pleasant, she'd also felt there was something about him she couldn't quite make out, something a bit mysterious, almost brooding. She had enough experience of men to see that this one looked as if he could be pretty tough if anyone upset him, and if that happened she would need plenty of back up.

Consequently Sally surprised Pat by turning up unexpectedly for the evening shift later that day. Sally considered mentioning the name Steve, just to see what reaction she got from her friend, but decided to wait and see if he came in again and, if he did, what reaction she saw from Pat. She must just be vigilant.

As the evening went by Sally stayed on the alert for any sign of Steve coming in. The place did get particularly busy in the evenings, hence the boss being quite happy for her offer of an extra pair of hands. But of course, with so many people coming and going, making it extremely difficult to keep her eye on just who comes and goes, and with a big demand for food, there are so many tables to wait on. Both girls, as well as two more, are kept rushing in and out of the kitchen with barely time to catch their breath, but even so, Sally makes a point of remaining vigilant.

She hadn't really thought just what to do if he did come in again while Pat was on shift. All she knew was that she felt the need to be there to help her friend if the need arose. Of course she may be wrong. This man may be looking for a different Annie altogether, but it did seem a coincidence that he should come out with the same name. All she could do was be there just in case to at least try to offer what protection she could.

Chapter Twenty.

As 'Pat', I find I prefer to be kept busy whenever possible, and have by this time decided to face up to the fact that I've got to face going it alone from now on. There would be no chance of help now. Why would he bother with me anymore, and if he were to be coming here I guess I would have seen him by now. Anyway, even if he had shown up what would happen? Would I be sure I'd be safe? I suppose, even now, part of me had been hanging on in Cambridge just on the hope he'd come looking for me and we could get back to how things were before, but bearing in mind the little amount I'd learnt from him before we split up, I know in my heart that I should probably keep on the move, but where to? That's the big question. I do so wish I knew what Steve would have done and where he'd have gone next.

"Service," the voice of the chef hits my ears, dragging me back to reality. I realise I've been daydreaming when I should have been working, and as the other girls are already busy I jump to and pick up the two dishes waiting to be taken.

"Table eight, in the corner, and watch where you're going," he says as I narrowly miss bumping into Sally who is hurtling into the kitchen in a particularly rushed pace!

"Is that for table eight," she asks, and before I can answer she takes it from me and rushes off as if there's some dire emergency to get it there quickly!

Now I know I've been daydreaming a bit tonight, but I can't imagine I'm so slow about my work. As she heads back toward the kitchen I notice her stopping to have a quiet word with the other two girls, but I'm not close enough to catch what she's saying. It seems to be something of interest as they both glance over in the direction of table eight, but from where I'm standing there is too much of a crowd to see round into that corner.

When they come back to the kitchen they bring with them trays of empty glasses and dirty dishes, and it seems they must be annoyed with me for some reason as it seems they've elected me to do the dishwasher while they carry on serving. I try not to show my annoyance, but I'm really not happy about it.

"Have I done something to upset you all?" I ask Sally eventually, "I feel you've all decided to keep me shut away in the kitchen all the time. And another thing, what's so exciting about table eight?"

"Oh no, sorry Pat, we're not upset with you at all. As for table eight, it's just some fellow off the street, nobody special. I think he's just going now anyway. Is the meal for table four ready yet?" Sally turns her attention to the chef, assuming she's smoothed over my frustrations for now.

Once again I feel my stubborn, inquisitive streak creeping to the surface. Why should I be kept in the dark

159

about things the other girls are sharing? I won't put up with it. I'll go and help out at the bar for a while, then I can see for myself some of the comings and goings. Without saying another word I stroll out through the door to the bar from where I can get a good look around, annoyingly not good enough to see past a group of lads standing between where I am and table eight.

I suppose they'll move eventually, so I get stuck into helping pull pints (a skill I only picked up in Birmingham!). Though I can see there's someone sitting there he has his back to me, and the lads keep moving around blocking my view. Oh well, I doubt I'm missing much so why bother? I'm just putting money in the till for the last drinks I've poured when the figure from table eight stands up….

Oh my God, it's him, it's Steve, though he's got his back to me I'm pretty sure it's him!

What should I do? What would he do if he saw me? Should I call out to him, rush over to him and ask him to forgive me? Or should I hide away, keep away from him so that he couldn't hurt me again? My mind is spinning, I can't think straight.

I feel a great rush of panic run through me. I just don't know what to do, so I do my usual cowardly thing and run without even waiting for him to turn round to be sure it is him! I make a sudden dash for the kitchen, so sudden that Sally and the other girls look shocked at my appearance. Judy, one of them, grins at me and asks, "What's up with you, rushing about so suddenly? Got one of the cheeky buggers touching you up?" I must look like a frightened rabbit!

"Leave her alone you, she's not as tough as you. Anyway Pat, I could do with your help over her for a bit plating up these last few orders. Chef's gone off duty and left us to finish off."

Part of me is relieved to have an excuse not to return to the bar, but there's also part of me that is wanting to sneak another look… just to see if it is actually him, or just someone who looks similar from behind. He was wearing a camouflage jacket like Steve wears, but then they are pretty common these days. What I can do I just don't know, but Sally seems to want me to stay where I am so perhaps I might never be sure either way? I suppose I could just ignore her and go back out there, but then if it was him what would I do? How would he react if he saw me? I wish I knew the answer to this question.

Judy and Kate are soon sent out to serve the last dishes while Sally keeps me in the kitchen to help clear up after the last one goes. She seems to be giving me rather a strange look, as if trying to read my mind, and a couple of minutes after the other two go out the room she turns round, looking me straight in the eye and says, "That's him, isn't it? The man who beat you up."

I try to look as if I've no idea what she means, "I tell you, I wasn't beaten up, I just…"

161

"Had an accident; I know, I've had 'accidents' like that with a man's fist before, remember. Sorry Pat, or is it Annie? I just don't believe a word of it. That one looks plenty tough enough to cause a fair bit of damage if you upset him too."

"It's not like that, it's like Judy says, he just tried to touch me up out there," I try to sound convincing, but can feel I'm not getting it over very well.

"You mean the chap on table eight don't you? The one calls himself Steve?"

I can feel her eyes piercing mine, looking for my reaction to the name, and this reaction is unmistakable. "Steve, did you say his name is Steve? How do you know that? Have you seen him here before? Where is he staying, has he asked about me?" My questions poured out in an unstoppable rush, like water from a tap, threatening to drown poor Sally in words.

She put her hand on my arm in an attempt to calm the flow and bid me to sit down and talk to her about it, not to do anything impulsive, but my mind was running its own course. Whatever she, or anyone else said right now, I knew I must see for myself if this really was my Steve. Regardless of what reaction I might get if it actually is him, I have to find out. I pull away from her and dash through the door to the bar, narrowly missing knocking Judy over in the rush, but when I get there and look around, table eight is vacant and there's no sign of him anywhere.

162

I ask the barman if he's seen the chap from table eight at all, but he tells me, "Yes, he was there a few minutes ago but left just after you went in the kitchen."

I must look somewhere between panic stricken and downright dejected, standing there in the middle of the pub, starring desperately at the door, begging it to open and bring him back in. In that brief instant I make a dash to the door and rush outside, looking up and down through the people out there in the hope to see him but, not knowing which way he went, I know it's useless attempting to find him out there in the dark. Anyway, I know how easily he manages to keep out of sight when he has a mind to. The question is of course, is he trying to find me, or trying to avoid me? Perhaps he's just passing through Cambridge. After all, he has no reason to expect me to still be here, even if he knew I came here in the first place. If he had been looking for me he might have thought I'd have done as he always taught me, and moved on some time ago.

Feeling miserable and totally dejected I went back to the kitchen, ignoring the odd looks from all those staff and customers who'd seen my dash out of the door! I was met by Sally at the kitchen door carrying my fleece. "Come on you, we're off duty now. The other two are finishing off so let's get out of here," and so saying she turned me about and marched me out the door.

I have to say I'm glad to get away from the staring faces around me. It's good to escape into the cool night air, and to disappear from there into the darkening streets. I don't want to be there where people are watching me, I just want to go back half an hour, I want to know if it really was Steve at table eight!

We walk in silence back through the market square, now like a skeleton of its daytime self, fleshless and without life. It was not until Sally had guided me firmly out from the city centre and toward the green space between there and the shelter that she finally speaks.

"Now are you going to tell me the truth about what happened? That was him wasn't it? You just can't keep defending him, if he could do that to you he could do it to others you know. You know what they say about leopards not changing their spots?"

"But you don't understand. Steve's not like that. You've spoken to him, did he sound threatening to you?" I ask her, in part hoping her answer will give me a clue about how he'd react if we did meet.

"No, I admit he didn't, he just gave me a lot of old soft soap and tried to convince me he was looking for his sister Annie who'd had a row with the boyfriend and run off. But anyone can make that up."

Desperately hoping to fit in with anything he'd said, and now feeling fairly sure he does want to find me, I tell her that he's right, I am his sister. To make the story more convincing and get her off my back about the bruises, I tell her that they were down to the boyfriend.

"He was awful! He just turned on me for no real reason and I panicked. I'm sorry for lying to you Sally, especially as you've been such a good friend to me. I should have told you the truth right from the start, but I was scared he'd come looking for me, and thought it would be better not to get anyone else involved. I never realised he had such a temper on him, but to be fair I did provoke him by doing something he'd specifically told me not to."

"Even so, there's no excuse for treating you like that, whatever you do. Right, so this Steve guy really is your brother then? So why did you dodge into the kitchen as if the devil himself was after you?"

Hopefully sounding convincing I tell her that I'd only seen the back of him through the crowd, and as they are the same build, and both wear similar jackets, I thought it was my boyfriend. To my relief she believed me!

We walked the rest of the way back to the shelter in silence, but what I really wanted to do was to run all over Cambridge in search of Steve, though I had to admit that Sally was right in saying we'd have more chance in the morning than out here in the dark.

"After all, we don't know if he's staying in a B&B or where."

If she knew Steve like I do she'd know he's more likely to be sleeping rough somewhere than anywhere he'd have to pay for!

Chapter Twenty-One.

The next morning I can barely manage to stay in bed past five o'clock. I think I've been awake most of the night anyway, and yet know it's no good going out looking for him until dawn. Wherever he spent his night he'll not surface until he thinks there's a chance of finding me… or at least, I hope that's what he still wants to do. Then of course there's still the slight worry in my mind that he is still looking for me with the intention of punishing me further for the way I'd behaved? Surely not. Of course that I'll not know until I find him, but I feel sure that if he still felt that bad about it he would be more likely to have just gone away as far from me as possible and left me to my own devises.

By the time Sally is about she finds me tucking into a quick breakfast of toast and coffee, ready and eager to rush out and scour the city. She kindly offers to come with me but, knowing this could make it awkward if we do find him, I suggest she just carries on as usual, does her lunch time shift at the pub, then if he should go there again she can tell him she knows where 'Annie' is, and will arrange for me to meet him later. That seems to make her happy but, before I go she makes me promise to be careful just in case 'that brute of a boyfriend' is about.

"Oh you don't need worry on that score, even if he is, if Steve's about he can sort that one," and as I say this I can't help doing a little inner chuckle to myself thinking back to that first night in Chesterfield with the druggies! Even so, I can't help feeling more than a little sad at the thought of poor Jake ever being referred to as a 'brute of a boyfriend'. There's no way he could or would ever have hurt me like Steve did, he was the total opposite in fact, and I still really wish I knew just what had happened to him.

I suppose in a way I probably wouldn't have stayed here in Cambridge so long but for two reasons. One was that Jake had brought me here on a couple of his business trips, and we really loved it. The other reason was of course, because I didn't know where else to go and was hoping Steve would come and rescue me.

Sally agreed to let me go off on my own on condition I stayed where there are other people about so that I'd be safe, just in case this imaginary boyfriend was out there, but I was actually quite relieved to set out alone on my search, just hoping he won't give up on me and leave before I find him. But just where to look I really don't know right now.

It's still fairly early and many of the street folk are still wrapped up in doorways and alleys, trying to keep warm until the day brightens up. It's difficult to know just how to tackle this. I can't really go around poking their sleeping bags to see who pops out. Well, I suppose I could but I'd risk getting a mouthful of abuse in most cases no doubt. Anyway, I can tell by the filthy condition of many that they're not Steve's. He may spend much of his life living rough but somehow he has never struck me as being dirty. In fact just the opposite which, now I come to think of it, is quite unusual for someone homeless. I'd not thought of that before; I assume he is homeless, either that or just a restless soul who prefers to keep on the move!

By the time I've done the rounds of the nooks and crannies of the night time city, Cambridge proper was coming to life. Those workers from shops, offices and tourist information places were pouring in from the outer provinces surrounding it. The market was gradually opening up with goods of all sorts being unloaded to bring new flesh to the empty skeleton we'd passed through last night.

"Hi Pat," a voice came through my thoughts and bringing me back to the present, "Any chance of a hand on the stall for an hour or so when I get set up? I need to dash up to get some fresh supplies. About eleven would be good if you could spare a while?"

It was Tom, the veg man. I've often helped him out with odd hours now and again, and normally I'd be pleased to, but today…? Oh well, I suppose you do get to see a fair number of people round the market, so I might as well come back around that time for a while and just keep my eyes peeled for any sign of Steve around there. "Ok Tom, I'll be back about then," and then as an afterthought I asked him if he could keep his eyes peeled for a man fitting Steve's description. "If you see him, and he says his name is Steve, can you tell him I'm looking for him so come here between eleven and twelve please?"

"You getting so desperate you have to go hunting men down now girl," Tom said with a laugh in his voice.

Little could I tell him that, yes, I am getting increasingly desperate to find this particular man, so I just laugh it off and kept walking. I spend quite some time roaming around a large shopping centre full of every kind of shop imaginable, most far too expensive for the likes of me… now that is. I remember Jake taking me into there to choose me an outfit for a dinner he was invited to. It cost a fortune, and made me feel drastically upmarket, mixing as we did that evening with top businessmen and their wives. I do remember feeling so amazing when I first dressed up in this outfit and walking in with my head held high. But by the time we'd been there for a while I realised that it wasn't the clothes that made the person, it was their manners, their personality, and most of all their common decency that made people worth bothering with! It took most of the women no more than half an hour to decide I wasn't up to their standard, after which they mostly turned their backs on me, leaving me feeling inferior, whilst meanwhile it took about the same time for most of the men to decide I was fair game! Poor Jake had been fuming when he realised what was going on, so we left early, leaving them the losers as he refused to do business with them after that and went elsewhere. Though I knew they got their comeuppance in the end, even now I shudder at the memory. To be fair probably the only bad one of Cambridge. All the other memories we made that week were good ones.

I roam aimlessly around for some time peering into shop windows, studying faces in the crowds, even walking up and down the queues of people waiting to climb on buses, hoping he hadn't already done so. By eleven o'clock I have had no luck and remembered I'd promised to help Tom out on the stall. I have to rush back to take over for him, and all I could do for just over an hour then is just to keep a close eye on the crowds milling about in the square. By the time Tom comes back and relieves me from my post I've more or less decided that Steve must have left the city after all, either on one of the earlier buses, or in one of the many other ingenious ways he has of moving around!

How I wish I hadn't fallen foul of him. Somehow he was so good at finding ways to get about, ways to survive, ways I just have not the slightest idea about. How on earth will I manage now?

At least the sun is bursting into life and producing what would be thought of as a perfect spring day, but it's certainly not going to be perfect as far as I'm concerned. My day is still overcast with the black cloud of misery, and I can find no escape, just an overbearing feeling of fear and depression. Fear that I don't know what to do or how to get myself out of this mess, and depression because I know I can't do that on my own.

I've decided to head back to the shelter to collect my things, knowing there's no more reason to stay here any longer, but first I'll pop into the pub for my last wages. I'll probably be needing them, even if I don't know what for right now. Reluctantly I say goodbye to Tom, though I decide not to tell him I won't be coming back. I do the same at the pub, once again saying nothing about leaving. I can't help looking around carefully at all the customers in here, just in case…, well you never know, he's been in twice, so he might have come back.

As I walk out the door I find myself standing there feeling totally lost once more. I know that as soon as I leave the shelter, worse still Sally, the only real friend I have right now, I'm genuinely on my own. Can I face her? She's been so good to me, but I know I can't tell her the complete truth, about the fact she's been helping a potential murderer! The silly part about it is that she would have no problem believing Steve was a murderer, but doubt she'd believe it of me, wimpish little me!!

I can't face walking back past the busy centre swarming with people, so I think I'll go the long way round. It'll take far longer, but what's the rush? It's not as if I have any plans. As I see it, it's a choice of getting on a bus, a train, or trudging off on foot, but where to? I've got absolutely not the slightest idea. Right now, if I could be where no one could see me, I would quite easily just sit down and howl, but I'd just draw attention to myself and look stupid. I can't help feeling just how easy it is to feel much lonelier in a crowd than on my own.

As I turn down a side alley in my attempt to find a quiet route back to the shelter, I stop to take one last look at the mighty King's College Chapel, a building I've always admired since the time Jake brought me here. I am not alone in my admiration as the whole of King's Parade on which it stands is packed with large groups of visitors, some gathered round listening to assorted guides who are trying their best to make themselves heard above one another.

Sadly I turn away and set off on my way. I'm just a few yards down the alley, feeling so very down, when I'm suddenly aware of music coming from behind me, coming from behind the masses of people I've just passed. I stop and listen, straining to hear above the general hubbub. It's obviously the sound of a busker such as there often is along there. I must admit, from this distance it sounds pretty good, so I stand for a few seconds listening.

Oh well, I better get going I suppose. I'm aware of the thought going through my head that if I were a dog I'd probably be sneaking off with my tail between my legs! Why do I have such stupid thoughts I wonder? Have I always been like this or is all to do with the bash on the head I'd had in that terrible cave what seems like a lifetime ago? I sometimes feel as if I barely know myself but then, if I don't who does?

Through the inane rush of stupid thoughts flying around my head I can still hear the busker playing back there in the distance. Something about it stops me in my tracks; I stand still for a second or two, straining to hear what it is about it that glued my feet to the ground, preventing me from walking off any further.

As I turn and go back a few yards to find out just what it is that's stopping me from walking off, I realise it's the tune, I've heard it before. As I walk slowly back a way to bring it to mind I remember what it is and where I heard it last. It's 'Stand by Me', and the last time I heard it was the day Steve performed it with Josh on the streets of Birmingham and in the pub karaoke.

The thought sends a shiver right through me. Could it be him? After all I know he was around here not so long ago. Perhaps he hasn't left after all. As I turn back and head the way I've come, I find myself confronted with a hoard of foreign folk who have no intention of moving out of my way. Normally I would be patient and let them by, but the nearer I get to the music, the more it sounds like Steve! I just know it's him. I fight my way through like a rugby player through a scrum, desperate to get to my goal before I miss it, miss him!

And there he stands, guitar in hand, playing and singing as if he did this every day, yet glancing around him as he does so, hopefully looking for me. I want to rush up to him and throw my arms round him, the relief is so great; but of course I still can't be one hundred percent certain of how he feels about me after Ely, and anyway, we've both been telling everyone that we are brother and sister, so I must act the part I suppose.

As I stand there with all these thoughts buzzing around my head, he looks straight at me, and I'm so relieved to see that same cheeky grin spread over his face, the one that has annoyed the hell out of me so often in the past. He doesn't stop playing but instead beckons me over, and before long it's clear he really does mean 'stand by me' as we sing the rest of the song together. Our duet seems to go down quite well with the crowd who are generous with their tips. The young man who had let Steve borrow his instrument was more than happy to share the proceeds, in fact would really like us to stay, but we had much to talk about, some of which could prove difficult, but I don't care, I'm not having to cope on my own anymore.

Chapter Twenty-Two.

At Steve's suggestion we buy a couple of packs of sandwiches and cokes and wander off in the direction of the river. Here we sit, leaning on a willow tree, so that we can talk in private and eat whilst we sit here. Though I say 'talk', just for a few minutes there's this uncomfortable silence between us. Neither of us seem able to decide how to start the conversation, yet I feel both of us have things to say.

Eventually the silence is breached by him handing me a sandwich and asking if I've managed to get plenty to eat since we parted company.

"Of course I have," I say with some indignation, "You don't think I've starved just because I've been on my own do you?"

"No. that's not what I meant. It's just that I've been worried about you, and didn't know where to find you Mel."

It was good to hear my real name again at last. From the time this nightmare started I'd been Jenny, then Annie, and since coming here I've been Pat, but I really miss being Mel.

"Steve, I…I just want to say…,"

"No Mel, don't. There's no need. It's me that needs to say sorry to you. I really had no right to treat you like that.

Do you reckon you could forgive me? More importantly, do you think you can trust me again?"

"It wasn't your fault. You told me not to follow you but I didn't listen. You had your reasons I'm sure, but it wasn't for me to question what you were doing. Can't we just forget it ever happened and move on, or would you prefer it if I leave you alone from now on?"

Just for an instant he sat quiet, staring straight ahead, before turning to me to say, "Yes, I did have my reasons, but I'd rather not talk about them right now … perhaps one day if that's ok, but that's still no excuse for what I did."

He looked for all the world like a child who's been caught misbehaving! Much as I wanted to push him on this I'd not the heart to do so nor, to be honest, the courage to take the risk, bearing in mind my knowledge of just what I now know from personal experience that he's capable of when pushed.

Sensing my lack of argument on this matter he turned to face me and said with something of his old glint in his eyes, "If you did leave me alone would you know what to do next; I've told you before you'd be useless on your own!"

In response to this remark I pull a rude face at him and throw the screwed-up sandwich wrapper at him. Thank goodness, it really begins to feel as if we're back on track, and I can feel safe in the knowledge that I'm no longer going to have to cope alone.

"So what've you been up to since you came here? I assume you found somewhere to put your head down?"

I explain to him about the shelter, it seems he did ask after 'Annie' there once, but Sally wasn't around and everyone else knew me as Pat. I explained to him about just how good she's been to me, befriending me when I needed it most, and finding me ways to earn enough to live on. It was then that I mentioned thinking I'd seen him in the pub, and how Sally had confirmed my thoughts after speaking to him the previous day.

"Hell, yes I do remember speaking to a girl in there, asking if she'd seen you. Why didn't she say then?"

"Seems she didn't believe your story about being my brother. Thought you were the boyfriend."

"What boyfriend is that," he asks.

"Well," I hesitate, then gingerly continue, "the one who beat me up. She saw the bruises." As I say this I'm not sure whether to look him in the eye or look away. The last thing I want to do is cause trouble just as we seem to be getting back on track, yet I knew that if he and Sally meet he needs to know the whole story the way I've told it to her.

For a few brief seconds Steve sits there with an inscrutable expression on his face before turning to me and saying, "That explains her attitude if she was suspicious of me. Do you reckon she accepted your story, or does she still know I'm a monster?"

"You're not a monster. I just pushed you too far. But if I promise not to do that again will you promise not to do what you did too?"

Looking me in the eye as if trying to read my mind, all he seems able to say is that he will do his best not to. I feel rather disconcerted at the lack of a firm promise on his part, but genuinely feel that, for whatever reason, he's concerned about his ability to control his temper. I wish I was brave enough to dig deeper into his past, into whatever makes him just who he is. Even so, I get the sense that 'his best' is going to have to do me right now.

"Anyway, have you been keeping an eye on the news lately?"

I have to admit I've not really bothered since coming here. Silly I suppose, but I think I've had bigger worries on my mind. Now Steve's brought it to my attention I find myself starting to panic again. "No, why, what's happened, are they on to us here?"

"Not exactly, so you can stop panicking. It's just that the police are widening their search to cover as far down as Birmingham, so it'll depend if anyone there recognises our description and reports us. Even then they'll have to find out where we've gone from there, so it gives us time to get right away from the area before they work it out."

I can feel panic taking over my brain, even though he's told me not to! "Where do we go now? What can we do to stay safe? Do they know we're together?"

"Didn't I just say not to panic? As for where to go, you just leave me to sort that one. They still seem unsure about whether you're on your own or have company. That's an ace up our sleeve. There are things we can do to help keep us safe. First, a trip to a chemist. Your hair is slowly going blonde again. I suppose the dye you used was a temporary one?"

I said it was, I'd had it done a second time in Birmingham but he was quite right, it was slowly fading back toward its original blonde colour. "Perhaps I'll go for purple or pink this time," I joke, but he was quick to clamp down on that idea, even if I had meant it.

Accordingly, we made a diversion into a chemist on our way to the shelter. Looking for all the world like a proper couple, we were just heading for the checkout with hair dye and toothpaste for me, and razors and shaving gel for Steve, when he stopped me,

"Here, try these on," he said, handing me a pair of off-the-peg glasses.

"Oh, now don't I look good in these, what do you reckon? I ask, looking at myself in the small mirror provided.

"I wasn't meaning to make you look good, just to make you look different," he mutters at me so the assistant can't hear.

"Ok, but what's wrong with it doing both things at once?" The look he gives me tells me that I was right in thinking we were back on track at last.

The last thing he buys me on our walk back is new hat. This one is pink and white with a pompom on top! It goes quite well with my grey fleece and I'm keen to wear it, but I'm given orders to keep both the hat and glasses until we leave here so they would act as a new disguise. For now Steve puts our purchases safely away in his rucksack, and we head off toward the shelter.

As we're crossing the green to get to the shelter I see the familiar figure of Sally ahead of us, so I call out to her to wait for us. I can't help noticing the slightly suspicious look in her eyes as I introduce her to 'my big brother Steve', any more than I can't help noticing the look he gives me at the thought of being my 'big' brother! But comparing myself with him I can't see how anyone can call him my little brother after all.

"Hello again Sally," he said, offering his hand to shake hers, Sis here tells me you thought I'd been knocking her about. I hope she's put you right about that?"

"Well yes, she did explain it to me when I saw her last night, but I have to admit I was on the verge of calling the cops on you when we first met, or even getting a few mates together to give you the beating she'd had before I met her."

"It's ok now though Steve, I've explained it was down to him, not you, so I reckon you're safe now." Not that I could ever imagine him not being safe, not unless her mates were particularly tough ones! The very thought makes me do an inner chuckle to myself once more.

We sit together on the very bench where I'd first met Sally, chatting away, me listening in awe of the smooth way he has of spinning her a very convincing tale of our home life, and how I'd picked up with a rather unsavoury character who had turned on me for no apparent reason. He explains that this is why I'd panicked and run away, but now he was here to take care of me.

"What if he comes after Pat, or should I say Annie?" she asks.

"Don't you worry about that, he won't come near her again." Somehow I could see she believes him now she's got to know him a bit, or at least, the bit he wants her to know!

The evening is turning cooler now and so the three of us head across the road to the shelter. Luckily there's room there for Steve as well, and a warm meal. This gives us time to chat a bit longer. Steve explains to Sally that we should really head back home tomorrow, "as our Mum is really worried about Annie", but we can stay for breakfast then look into buses or trains. He tells her we are heading up to Durham (where does he get that idea from I'd like to know!).

"You don't sound as if you come from that part of the country," She says.

"No, you're right. We only moved there recently to get away from the hustle and bustle of London. Now Mum's on her own we decided to go there with her as that's where her family are from."

Hell, this man's good at a pack of lies; very convincing lies at that! Probably make a brilliant politician I think.

When we decide to turn in for the night Sally tells us she's doing an early shift helping chef prep in the pub kitchen in the morning. "So I might not be here when you leave, so I'd better say goodbye now."

We hugged a really meaningful hug, and I thanked her for having been such a good friend when I needed one most. I was pleased to see Steve also giving her a warm, big brotherly hug too, before she disappeared off to her bed leaving me, once again, crying into his shoulder, making it damp yet again.

As Sally had predicted, she was up and gone before we met for breakfast. By the time we'd eaten there was nobody about as the ladies providing the breakfast were busy in the kitchen. Steve suggested that this might be a good opportunity for me to set to with the hair dye so no one would notice.

"We can be out of here before we see anyone who knows you."

I don't think he quite expects to see me with auburn coloured hair, I wasn't too sure myself at first. But now it's dry and put into some sort of style, I think I can get used to it.

I'm going to miss Sally, and to a point, miss being here in what's been my temporary home for a while. Perhaps I'll come back one day. I have asked Steve if I could leave some sort of contact details for Sally, but he was adamant that this would be a big mistake, so I'll just have to come back one day for sure.

As we head off to the bus station I'm finally allowed to don both my new glasses, and my new pink and white hat as the weather is rather fresh right now, and I must admit they do make me feel like a whole different person.

"Where to now?" I ask Steve.

"Not sure yet, just be patient and I'll see."

And that was all he said, so I'll just have to wait and see!

Chapter Twenty-three.

It seems he really doesn't know exactly where to go next, but little things like that don't seem to faze him in the slightest. Does anything much I ask myself? And yet of course, on those rare occasions when something does, the consequences can be pretty sudden and pretty ferocious. Even so, I can't help feeling safer with him around than without him. After all, I still have no idea how I came to be in that awful cave and, worse still, why I'm being accused of murdering my dear Jake. There must obviously be a connection between the two things but I just don't understand what that is, or how to escape this nightmare situation I'm in.

I know somehow that Steve is probably my only hope of finding a way out of this mess, so whatever he decides and wherever he says we should go, that's got to be my best chance of surviving this. Having said this I find myself feeling somewhat useless, trotting along with him like a pet dog as usual, and waiting to be given commands.

At the bus station I find myself standing quietly amongst the crowds of passengers whilst Steve walks up and down checking out the destinations of the different buses lined up, or the timetables for those not yet in. This seems to be an extremely busy time of day, making it hard to keep my eyes on him through the crowds around us. Suddenly, to my horror, I notice a policeman coming toward me! I strain my ears to hear what he's asking other people and am shocked when I realise he's showing them a picture and asking if they'd seen this girl. I'm even more shocked when I realise that the picture he's showing them is actually of me! Ok, me with long blonde hair, but me none the less. Help! What on earth should I do now, make a run for it, or stand still and accept the consequences? Somehow something tells me that running would be the worst thing to do under the circumstances.

Steve, where's Steve when I need him? As I look down through the early morning crowds waiting there, I see him. Just as the policeman gets to me I am aware of Steve trying his hardest to fight his way through to get to me but not before I find myself looking at myself and being asked if I'd seen this person!

What should I do, what can I say? Think Mel, I tell myself, stop panicking as Steve would say. Then, almost without giving it any thought, I found myself smiling sweetly at him and coming out with,

"Pardonnez-moi monsieur, ici pour render visite a ma cousine. Je parle un pue anglais."

I reckon I was as shocked as this poor bobby who obviously knew even less French than I thought I knew, and accepting that and the shake of my head as a negative answer to his question, and not wanting to look too ignorant, he thought better of bothering further with this enquiry. Just as he walked away Steve managed to get through to me and shepherded me straight onto the nearest bus without so much as a word spoken. Obviously he'd overheard the interaction between myself and the poor young bobby, and was keen to get me away before he came back with a French speaking colleague.

"What the hell was that?" he muttered quietly as the engine started up, "I didn't know you could speak French."

"Ah, you see, you don't know everything about me do you," I enjoyed for once not being an open book. It felt good just for a minute to have a little mystery about me rather than him.

"No, I suppose I don't. But then you don't really know much about me either though, do you."

He was certainly right about that. In fact since we met I've always found that every time I've learnt something new about this man, I've found it's always outweighed by more things that I don't know.

Now here we are on a bus to somewhere, though where I have no idea, with no definite plan as to where we're going or why. Though I say this I realise it's conceivable that Steve does know, but is just keeping it to himself, so I'll just have to wait and perhaps he'll fill me in eventually. Anyway, at least now I do have the comfort of knowing I'm no longer alone, and that is a big relief to me.

We haven't travelled far before he breaks into my reverie by announcing we need to get off the bus. I can't believe we're getting off so soon. "Why, where are we? Is this as far as we needed to go? I would have thought it wasn't worth getting on for that distance, might almost have been as easy to walk."

"You… walk? I can see I must be having some good effect on you, even if it's just to get you fitter."

"Don't kid yourself it's your influence doing that. I'm sure I've always been reasonably sporty anyway, even before I met you," I say this jokingly, even if I've no real certainty about it either way. But then, you never know, perhaps I was a top sports woman of some sort in my past life!

"Oh yes, is that why you had a job keeping up with me when we had to walk, then needed a shove to climb onto those hay bales? What sort of sport do you reckon you're good at?"

"I'm not sure at the moment, but I'm sure it'll come back to me, just like everything else will in time." As I say this I can't help thinking how I wish 'everything' would come back to me sooner rather than later. Though much of it has I feel I should be able to throw some light onto Jake's demise, but I draw a complete blank on that front.

"Hey, what's up you?" Steve is standing there looking me in the eye, "What are you worrying about now?"

I can see there's no way I can fool him by fobbing him off with some casual answer, so I tell him my worries about not remembering a thing about the murder.

"Did I do it, do you think? Has my mind just blanked it out, and that's why I don't remember?

Without saying a word he took my hand, put it over his arm, and led me away from the odd people still at the bus stop, and across the road, over a stile, and into a nearby field. There was obviously a footpath running through here but clearly not much used, so it wasn't hard to put his jacket down for us to sit on when we reached the far side, away from other people.

"Now," he said in a firm but gentle tone of voice, "Just you listen to me. No, I do not think your mind is blanking out the murder. I've listened to what you've said so far, and I've got to know you pretty well, and I think I can honestly say that the reason you don't remember anything about the murder is simply because you weren't there at the time! You said yourself that Jake was alive the last time you saw him, and I believe you. Besides," he adds with a broad grin on his face, "you haven't got it in you to kill in cold blood, have you?"

Though this is his way, adding this last remark really winds me up and I can't help but feel that at least I still have one person who has faith in my innocence, all I can hope is that there is some way to prove it to everybody else. Until then I'm going to stick to him like glue, trusting that he will be able to find a way out for me.

Resisting the temptation to say that I might make an exception in Steve's case, I reluctantly agree that I couldn't imagine murdering anyone, least of all my Jake. I opened my mouth to ask casually, could he do so…but somehow the words stuck. Perhaps it would be an awful thing to admit to, but after seeing his 'other' side, something inside me warned me off from asking the question even in jest, as I really believe if driven to it he would certainly be capable of doing this! I make a mental note never again to push him anywhere near such lengths.

Though we were not so far from Cambridge, apparently due to the need to leave so suddenly, regardless of direction, Steve decided it was as good a time as any to have another delve into my rather tatty memory. Though it was so much clearer now I wasn't too sure how much I could offer that would be of use, but that didn't seem to bother him. We'd brought a couple of bananas and some apples that I'd been given yesterday by Tom, so while we talked we ate a banana each by way of a snack.

As we sat there eating these Steve asked me to tell him all I could remember about Jake, his family, friends, business and of course, about our relationship.

"Just relax and tell me anything that comes to mind. Doesn't matter how big or small the stuff you think of. Just anything so I get a clearer picture of him. For a start, he must have been a brave chap to take you on," said with that damn grin again!

"Huh! I'll have you know he was pleased to have me." Then, letting my mind drift back to the beginning of our relationship, I thought I should quantify this statement just a tad.

"When we first met I had been out a few times with his brother, Andy. I knew he had talked about having an older brother, Jake, but for some months I never got to meet him. All I knew was that he was some sort of techno nerd, but that really didn't mean much to me. Though he was a sort of junior partner, Andy was more into sports of one sort and another, so they didn't spend so much time together outside the office on the whole."

"Did you meet their parents at all? Were they a well-off family do you think, or was it just Jake who made the money?"

"I did meet them once, but they weren't impressed. Thought I wasn't good enough for their son, not educated enough! Apparently Jake and Andy had both been to a private school, then on to university. All I did was go to an ordinary secondary school and a short time at the local college. His father was a retired, high ranking army officer, but that didn't seem to bother either of their sons."

"So what made you change brothers' mid-way then? Or were they into sharing their toys like good little boys?" I might have expected some sarcastic remarks as I relay my story, but this one, though I tried to look annoyed, did rather amuse me.

"Will you keep your remarks to yourself and just listen if you want me to go on?"

"Sorry, promise I'll do as my granny used to tell me when I was a lad, and hold my tongue!"

"Bet you didn't take a blind bit of notice of her either?" I retaliate.

By this time we were both feeling completely relaxed sitting here. The spring sunshine was soaking into us both, and I for one am in no rush to get up and move on. For a while we sit quietly enjoying the peace and quiet of the Cambridgeshire countryside.

After a while Steve broke the silence to ask how I came to change from one brother to the other, especially as Andy sounded easy-going, and Jake was that bit older.

"That's not the first time I've been asked that question," I tell him, "I sometimes wonder about that myself, but it was Andy who introduced us that time when he took me for a visit to see his parents. I'd been dreading it, as you can imagine, but he couldn't understand why I was looking on it as an ordeal to be faced. Somehow he didn't see the way his mother looked down her nose at me that day. Neither did he seem to see how uncomfortable I felt being grilled about my own background by his father." I can still wince at the thought of that first meeting!

"Anyway, we'd been there for the best part of an hour when I decided to make some excuse and leave. Problem was that I couldn't think of any particularly suitable ones! To be honest, I was really struggling to cope with his mother's constant interrogation, or that's what it felt like, but of course Andy couldn't seem to see it. Just as I was thinking of making a total fool of myself and making a run for it, Jake walked in. My first thought was that this must be their number one son, the one I expected to be even snootier than the parents."

"And was he?"

"No, not at all. He'd only been in the house five minutes before he realised what I was having to put up with. I was never more relieved than when he offered to show me round the garden. Andy, by then, was busy on the phone to a mate, so I was glad to accept the way out."

I explain to Steve how much more attentive Jake was than his younger brother that day. "Even so, I must admit that I really didn't take to him as easily as I had Andy. A while after that I was at a party with Andy when Jake came in. I found it aggravating the way he seemed to attract girls 'like bees round a honey-pot' as the saying goes. He hardly seemed to notice though, but I soon realised Andy was the one who tended to be a bit fickle. I'd find him chatting up someone new at every do we went to, usually leaving me on my own. That's when Jake saw what was happening and stepped in. By then Andy seemed quite happy for his brother to take on his left-offs!" This seemed to amuse Steve no end, the thought of me being a 'left-off'. I suppose, put like that, there is a funny side to it.

"As I say, at first I didn't like him that much, probably because he could be a bit intolerant of people who spent their time trying to impress him just because he had money, and I felt that made him a bit cold at times."

"So what changed your mind, or should I ask, what persuaded him to take you on? He must have been either a brave man or a fool, and from what you say he was no fool."

Looking back on the early days of our relationship I realised I've never given thought to just why Jake liked me, it was just something that had grown on us both until we knew it was meant to be. Now I did think back to the beginning I can honestly say that, as I now tell Steve, it all came about because I had once accused him of flashing his money around and trying to look big, when he'd offered to pay a bill in a bar for me one day. I'd been out with a couple of friends to celebrate my birthday, and when I went to pay the bar tab found myself considerably short of funds!

Of course I knew who he was but, partly because I knew he was Andy's rich big brother, and partly because I'd had a few too many drinks, instead of accepting his offer gracefully, I found myself calling him a 'flash git', telling him 'I don't need your money', and trying to make a quick getaway but falling flat on my face before making the door!

My relaying of this story has the effect of sending Steve into complete meltdown. It's typical of him to get such fun at my expense. When he eventually manages to control his laughter he wipes the tears of laughter off on his sleeve and says,

"So I see your Jake did share that trait with me; we both seem to like taking on a challenge! I doubt he'd ever had anyone tell him to keep his money before, let alone a girl who would do that then fall at his feet all in the same breath!"

I do my best to give him my best withering glare, not that it has any noticeable affect as he's still trying to fight back the last tears of laughter. Even so, I must admit that, looking back on it, I must have caused much amusement in the bar that night. I believe I only ever went back there after that when I was with Jake, and no one dared bring the subject up again, though they must have laughed about it behind my back.

Anyway, because of the state I was in he drove me home that night, but was so good. He made no attempt to take advantage of me, but just flopped me down on the sofa, found a blanket from upstairs to cover me up, and left.

"Now I know Andy would certainly not have been so trustworthy. He was the sort to have taken advantage of any sort and at every opportunity, even of his own brother come to that. I think that was when I realised I felt so much happier with Jake, because he always made me feel safe...sort of protected, in a way that Andy never did."

As I tell Steve this I can't help but think that perhaps, though not in quite the same way, he too has in so many ways and on so many occasions also made me feel safe and protected.

Chapter Twenty-Four.

At this point the sky is becoming very overcast. I can see heavy looking rain clouds moving in our direction. We pick up the jacket we've been sitting on and start heading off, though where to I've no idea. I rarely bother to ask these days as I know I have no say in the matter so just keep tagging along! I'm never sure if Steve really has any set plan or just makes it up as we go along, but anything is better than being on my own as I'd been recently, an experience that's taught me that my best hope is to put my trust in him and pray for a good final outcome to my nightmare.

We seem to have left the bus at a stop well out of town, obviously at a stop designed to serve a quiet, pretty village. There are some assorted cottages, some tiled but many thatched roofs, and of course the obligatory village pub. Almost by design, just as we pass this the heavens open and, by chance, so does the pub. Having spent so long sitting around talking I'd not noticed just how late in the morning it is, but I'm more than pleased to find my companion steering me in through the door and out of the torrent dropping from the sky outside. We must have looked particularly desperate as the landlord was back behind the bar before the rain fell, and so hadn't realised that it was his roof as much as his refreshment we were so eager to have!

I can't help thinking he looked somewhat disappointed when we ordered two cups of coffee, but his face brightened up a little when I suggested to Steve that we should have a couple of the tasty looking sausage rolls he had on display on the bar.

"Good choice young lady," he said, "They're fresh and straight out of the oven, so good and warm for a wet day." By this time he could not only see the rain through the windows, but could hear it hammering on the roof of the porch through which we'd just come. I really enjoy the combination of the warm roll washed down with a good hot coffee whilst we sit in a cosy corner and continuing the conversation from a while ago.

"So you've said that Jake had business associates who he'd upset?" I nodded in reply to this and said I don't really know just who to suggest though. "Did he have any actual partners or others who you think would gain if he wasn't...there?"

I know he was trying to avoid saying 'dead' for my sake, as we're out of earshot of the landlord. I have to admit I don't really know the names of most of them as I was never involved with them if I could help it. "He did have a handful of good, loyal staff and some of those well up in the company were pretty well thought of by him, but he was always suspicious of anyone too pushy and eager to climb the ladder as it were. As I said before, Andy and a chap called Brooks, Tony Brooks, were partners, but Jake held the larger share."

"So Andy did work with him? Would he gain by the loss of his brother?"

"Although he took Andy into partnership with him I think that, to be honest, he really wasn't up to much according to Jake, so he got brought in in a lesser capacity, just to keep their parents happy I think. Bit of a token gesture really."

"So presumably he could be in line to take over the firm with the right people running it with him, this Brooks character for instance, to say nothing of him being heir to a larger share of their parents' riches one day?" It was clear to see Steve's reasoning. I'd not looked at it that way until now. It does seem an obvious possibility, but it's a frightening thought that Andy would even consider killing his brother for money.

"Perhaps he was tired of living off the scraps from big brother's table. Think we need to eliminate him first. Where does he live?"

"With his parents of course, that means he gets the best of both worlds. Looked after by mummy and daddy, and funded by big brother of course," I tell him. Then on reflection I can't help asking Steve, "When you say to 'eliminate him' you don't mean ... "

"What do you think I mean stupid? Eliminate him from our enquiries, not from the world for goodness sake!"

I know I shouldn't even have thought that was even a possibility, but there are still odd occasions when I look at him and see a stranger deep inside of the man I think I know. As he says though, I'm just being stupid, even to suspect it of him.

"So do we head for their place next? I think I can remember where it is now."

"No, 'we' don't. You point me in the right direction then keep out of sight. The last thing we want is for them to know you're about, especially Andy if there's even the slightest chance of him being involved."

I can't stress enough just how pleased I am to hear Steve say that. Certainly, if there's a suspicion I'm to blame for Jake's death, there's no way I could face his parents. I hope in a way that Andy is as innocent as I am even though he was a bit of a leach where his rich brother was concerned, but he did have a rather endearing side to him when he cared to show it, and in some respects he had felt a bit like a brother to me once I was with Jake instead of him.

Even so, I suppose Steve is quite right in suggesting checking him out first. After all, he did have plenty to gain from the loss of Jake. I just can't see him actually doing the deed himself, but I suppose he could have employed a hit man!

Before too long the rain clears up, leaving a sky so clear it's difficult to believe it had ever rained except for the puddles here and there as we set off once more on our journey. The warmth we gained from the coffee and those lovely sausage rolls was enough to get us off to a good start. This time I don't bother asking about our destination as I know I'll not get any satisfaction in that quest. All I do know is that, if we are heading for the Marden household in Richmond, we have an awfully long way to go. Surely he's not planning on us doing it all on foot!

I try suggesting that perhaps we should be out on one of the bigger roads to give us chance of a lift, but as Steve quite rightly says, hitching a lift on a motorway (because that's what it would be), is not only dangerous, but would put us out on view for all to see, especially police.

"We'll take a little stroll for a while and see if we can find a lift from somewhere less visible further down the road." A 'stroll' he calls it! I'll believe that when I see it.

We walk on for nearly an hour before entering another village, and it's as we do so that we stop to take a few sips of water from our water bottles. Only then do we realise that we'd forgotten to fill them before setting off that morning.

"How do we manage now," I ask, feeling more than a little guilty as I believe he had asked me to see to that job.

"There looks like a park of some sort over there. Perhaps there's a tap we can use. Let's go and see."

We walk round into the park but can't see a tap. There's a woman across the far side walking her dog, a beautiful almost white retriever, and one who obviously enjoys all the attention she can get. While I squat down responding to her request for affection (the dog, not the owner!), Steve explains our predicament over lack of water, blaming me for my neglect.

"That's no problem. There is a drinking fountain over there in the corner of the play area. I'm sure you can use that for a refill. If not I only live across the road, so you're welcome to come back with me for a refill."

"That's really kind of you, but I'm sure we can do it over there now you've been kind enough to point us in the right direction thanks," he says in his best flirty voice!

He managed to fill both bottles from the water fountain there and, while we sat with the lady and her dog on a low wall, he quizzed her as to directions from here, telling her that we were planning eventually to reach the outskirts of London.

"You've got an awful long way to go then," she said, "why don't you go to the industrial site at the end of the village and see if you can scrounge a lift some of the way?"

"That sounds a good plan, is it far away? Would you mind pointing us in the right direction please?" I can't help thinking just how smarmy can he get, but of course it has the right effect on the poor woman. Consequently the three of us and the big white dog head off toward the road, where she points us in the direction we need to go and wishes us luck. As we disappear round the corner, I look over my shoulder and see her standing where we'd left her, waving to us. I wave back to her and at the same time nudge Steve and tell him it's him she wants a wave from. He duly turns and waves as I've suggested. Wow! That's a first. He never usually listens to anything I suggest.

Sure enough we come across a small industrial estate just around the corner. I think Steve has hoped to sneak, unnoticed into the back of one of the vehicles there but it's not looking very hopeful. To be totally honest I wonder just where we're going to expect to go from here if we get a lift, but Steve seems quite confident that there must be someone going south at least, so it's worth a try.

There's an assortment of units on the estate, many with vehicles of one sort or another outside, either loading or unloading goods. I suggest to him that it might be wise to ask which ones are going our way but, quite wisely I suppose, he says he would prefer not to make ourselves noticed if we could avoid it.

Unfortunately it seems we're out of luck as far as sneaking into any of these as they are all locked, except those who actually have someone still loading them. I can see what's coming next, and I'm soon proved right!

"Oh well, looks like another little stroll. Come on then you, best foot forward."

We've only just gone a few yards out of the site when there's a hoot of a car horn behind us. I look round and see a car coming up behind and stopping parallel to us.

"Hello again," it was the lady we'd met earlier with the dog, "I don't know which direction you need to go, but I'm going to pick up a friend from Stansted airport, and can drop you off down there somewhere. You might be able to pick up a lift at the services there."

"That's so kind of you," he says, once again throwing her his best smile, and before I get the offer he climbs straight in beside her and I'm left sitting on the back seat! Of course, he'll probably tell me it's to save me being recognised, but I know it's just to annoy the hell out of me by chatting her up! All I can do is smile sweetly and speak when I'm spoken to, though with him next to her that's not very often. She's obviously quite smitten with him, and he's really playing up to it!

It's difficult to catch everything that's said from the back seat, but I gather we're playing the brother and sister game again, only this time it seems I'm Pat. I can't help wondering if I'll ever get to be Melanie Cook again, or must I spend my life reinventing myself? I have to say that I'm still not completely sure I know exactly who I am even now, though my mind seems to be completely recovered from what's happened before, but it's just so hard to take in all that seems to have happened or is still happening to me. I'm sure my life was pretty ordinary and straight forward before, but now I'm just living from day to day, minute to minute. I can't help wondering if things will ever get back to normal, if there is such a thing as normal!

Our kind new friend, true to her word, takes us all the way to Stansted Airport where she is meeting a friend. Before she leaves us she points us in the right direction for the coaches to London, though having roamed about so much of late I feel sure we would have had no problem finding this! We said our goodbyes, one of us that bit more gushingly than I feel was necessary (just in an attempt to aggravate me), and head off for the ticket office. It is not much more than half an hour later that we we're on the coach heading for Stratford on the outskirts of London.

Chapter Twenty-Five.

In just under an hour we found ourselves alighting from the coach and making our way towards the nearest burger bar. It seemed ages since we last ate, and that had not been sufficient to fill us up, so I could barely keep my stomach from making embarrassing noises on the coach. I can never figure out how it is that Steve never seems to have problems coping with hunger, perhaps he's used to going for long spells without food, but it's clear that I'm obviously not in that habit.

"What do we do now then," I ask, "Are we safe here? What do we do and where do we go next?"

He can see straight away that I'm feeling more on edge as we get closer to where Jake's business, and more importantly, his house is. I've no idea if he has a plan or is just playing it by ear, but I'm beginning to wish I was still miles away. As we sit here eating he gently quizzes me as to just where both places are. Reluctantly I agree to show him where Jake's office was, on condition I don't have to go in, or even too close come to that.

"No, I just want to get a picture of the man, and how he lived his life. You say Andy worked with him?"

"Not sure worked was the right word but, yes after a fashion I suppose, though when it came to getting too involved Brooks did more than him I believe. That meant he didn't have to work so hard to earn a living. Andy always seemed content to live off the profits from his brother's labours, as long as it didn't involve working too hard! Sweet as he was at times, he was by no means ambitious.

The next question Steve came up with was about where was their parents' home. "That's out in Richmond area, you know, where the posh folk live. I suppose you want me to take you there too do you?"

"No, you won't need to do that. Andy can do that," and seeing the shocked look on my face he casually explains that he has a plan to get a better look at the family and find out just what's going on from their viewpoint.

"You won't tell them where I am will you? I bet they believe it was me like the police suspect. They had me labelled as a gold-digger, but I wouldn't have cared if Jake had been poor. It wasn't his money I was after, in fact it was his money that nearly kept us apart when I thought he was a 'flash git'. He knew that too because he said he was sick of women chasing him for his money."

"Don't worry, I won't mention you. They won't even know who I am, just some bloke Andy is about to meet. Anyway, let's get walking. I reckon we need a good hour to get near the area you say the office is. We should be able to find a room in a hostel near there with any luck, then I can get cleaned up for a night on the town while you bed down for the night."

I can't for the life of me understand just what he has in mind, but then I'm getting to accept that now almost without question, or at least not much. By just over an hour we have found a cheapish hostel, bearing in mind our diminishing funds, and established ourselves in a sparse but clean room with sufficient furniture to serve as a temporary base. I must admit to feeling just slightly shocked on this occasion when I hear Steve book us in as Mr and Mrs Lockett! That's the first time we've been more than brother and sister since that day back in Derbyshire. It didn't seem to mean much back then as we hardly knew each other at that point, but now, after spending so long together, it did seem to carry a whole different significance to it.

"You do realise there's only one bed in here," I point out to him as he closes the door behind us.

"Don't get on your high horse 'Mrs Lockett', you can have it all to yourself, I'm going to have a clean-up and then I'm out of here. You can have a quiet night in front of the tv and get a good night's sleep. If I get back in time I'll use my sleeping bag."

So saying he grabs his wash bag and clean clothes from his rucksack and disappears into the tiny on-suite. When he reappears I can hardly believe the difference. He looks a whole new man, clean, fresh and well-trimmed facial hair, nothing like the rough-sleeper I picked up with all that time ago, in fact almost presentable! He's wearing a new shirt and jeans I've not seen before, which he tells me came from cash he'd earned doing shifts at a car wash while looking for me in Cambridge. It had never occurred to me before to ask how he'd come by the money he'd been living on back then.

"Right, I'm off out. Don't wait up for me wifey!!"

He just manages to duck as I sling one of his smelly old shoes at him. Then he's gone.

Oh well, I think I'll follow suit and have a quick shower, I certainly feel the need today. At least now I know he's gone off I can do so in privacy. We may be pretending to be a couple, but that doesn't extend to shower sharing.

I check first that the door is firmly locked before stripping off, turning the shower on, and jumping straight in… swiftly followed by jumping straight out again! Damn the man, he's only used up all the hot water! I wrap myself in the large white towel provided and wait stretched out on the bed to figure out how the tv works while the water heats up just enough to jump in and out quickly, before donning my pyjamas (also acquired whilst at Cambridge) and wriggling in under the covers, feeling warm and surprisingly relaxed.

I think I vaguely remember turning the tv off just before I dropped off to sleep. I believe the clock on the wall had said just gone eleven then, and I probably went straight off to sleep.

"Get away, leave me al…" I scream out, but my scream is stifled by a firm hand over my mouth!

"Ssh Mel, it's just me, Steve."

I look up into that face I now know so well and bite back the eruption of tears I can feel rising up like a volcano inside me.

"God, you're shaking girl, I didn't mean to scare you, come here," he says as he puts a gentle arm around my shoulders to calm me. It takes some few minutes to even stop the shaking. I don't know why it's hit me so hard, but perhaps because I was thinking about Jake before I dropped off last night, and how close we were now to where I'd shared his house with him for the past months, and I remember having visions of him lying dead on the floor there with the murderer standing over him!

When I do manage to collect my self composure I glance up at the clock again. "It can't be nine o'clock, you only left at eight," I say, trying to figure out why my brain doesn't seem to be functioning properly.

"You're right, I did go out at eight, but that was last night. It's nine a.m. now."

"Do you mean to say you've been out all night?"

"That's right, Sort of lost track of time. That Andy of yours is a real party animal isn't he? And those snobby parents. Phew! I can quite see why you didn't like them. Don't reckon they liked me any more than they did you as it happens only in as much as I was kind enough to take their 'baby boy' home to them safe and sound. Well, that's if you call him being totally out of it safe and sound!"

"Oh hell Steve, what have you been up to? I wasn't expecting you to get as close as that to them. How did you do it?"

"That was easy enough. I waited outside the place where you showed me he worked and followed him. I figured from what you said he was the sort who'd go to the nearest bar before going home to Mummy and Daddy, and that's just what he did, so I followed him in and chatted him up a bit. I reckon the reason your boy couldn't commit to one woman is because he'd rather commit to a man, if you get my drift."

"No, you don't mean ...? Surely not? But then, come to think of it that would explain a lot. I wonder if Jake knew and that's why he was happy to take me off him. But whatever would his parents say if they knew?"

"I think at least the old man knows, but is working on the theory that if you ignore it, it'll go away, or perhaps he'll grow out of it one day!"

"So you really did get to meet his parents too? How the hell did you pull that one off?"

Steve gave a good hearty laugh before explaining to me,

"Well you see, we had, or at least he had, a real heavy nights drinking. Bless him, he poured his poor, pathetic heart out to me. He was in no state to drive home, so I ordered a cab and delivered him there. Mummy darling was so grateful she invited me to stay the night."

"Not in the same bed I hope?" I couldn't resist that one, "Didn't they blame you for his condition?"

"No, do I look that sort. I prefer my own company in bed thanks. No, they didn't seem to blame me. I think they're either used to it, or they put it down to grieving for his brother."

If that is the case then my next question pretty well answers itself. Still, I need to know, I need to find out who would do such a thing as to kill my Jake. I hesitate before allowing the words to come out, somehow just speaking them makes it all seem so much more real now we're down so close to home.

"So, did you get chance to make a clear judgement about him? Do you think there's any chance it could have been him that killed Jake?"

"No, no way, he's too much of a wimp; and besides, he had no real motive. From what I could get out of him they were quite close as brothers go, and he seemed to have had no ambitions to take on the business. In fact just the opposite. All the time he tagged along on Jakes shirt tails, as you suggested, he gained much by doing little and was happy to do so. Now he's going to have to work harder or sell up to one of the partners and get a proper job."

"So what next, where do we go from here? I suppose you want me to take you to our house next do you?"

"I will eventually, but first I'm meeting up with Andy to get the lie of the land as regards the business set-up. He kindly offered to show me round later today, so it'll give me chance to get to meet a few other possible suspects. Do you know who'd be likely to top our list, anyone you think would have a particular motive?"

All I can do is attempt to go over the list I made previously of the few names I can remember, though with most it's just first names. I didn't go there more than a handful of times, and even then I tended to stand in the background while Jake spoke to them about work. It was far too technical for me to understand, even if I'd wanted to.

As we talk over my rather scant memory we sit on the bed with a cup of tea I've made, and eat an unusual breakfast of bacon baps and crisps Steve had brought back with him. It seems, to my chagrin that Mrs Marden had insisted he had a good full English before he left, I suppose in return for bringing her son home the night before. Even so, he still manages to help me clear off the baps and crisps!

Though I have managed to come up with a few names, there are none on this list truly strike me as either benefiting from Jake's death, or even less being capable of causing it. While we sit eating Steve put on the tv to catch the weather forecast as he says we'll be outside a lot this week. What we hadn't counted on is that we'd just catch the tail end of the news too.

'The search is still on for Melanie Cook, in connection with the murder of her fiancée Mr Jake Marden. There were suspected sightings of her in the Chesterfield area some weeks ago, but these have not been confirmed. It was believed that she was attempting to make her way to Ireland via Liverpool but there has been no confirmation of this. There has also been a search using police dogs across part of the Peak district to the south of Macclesfield, but that proved inconclusive. Since then there have been no further sightings though it seems possible that she has been joined by an accomplice, but so far no description has been released.'

"Oh my God, They're onto us Steve. They know you're with me. They're bound to catch up with us now surely?"

"Here you go again! Give over woman and eat your breakfast. Didn't you hear what they said? The last positive sighting was Chesterfield, from there on its just speculation. Let's face it, we're miles from there and have been for some time now, so they've got a way to go to catch up with us yet."

"Yes but they know about you being with me… "

"You'll get indigestion if you keep fussing like that when you're eating. What they actually said, if you'd listened instead of panicking, is that it's 'possible' that you have an accomplice. Even if they suspect it, they have no real proof or they'd give out a description. Now give us another handful of those crisps will you and save your panic for when they really have something positive to go on."

I'd throw something at him, but the only thing available is my pillow, and I'm too comfortable leaning on it right now, so I have to make do with just throwing him a filthy look for always making me feel such a wimp! Well I suppose we've got this far without getting caught, so he's probably right. Even so, surely the fact that we're so close now must make it more risky than before. I realise he seems totally relaxed about the whole situation but, even though I now trust him totally, I can't help feeling jittery from time to time. After all, wouldn't anyone after being labelled a murderer?

Chapter Twenty-Six.

"So what do I do while you go gadding about with your new mate Andy then? I guess I'm not coming with you?" Really meaning I hope I'm not of course.

"No, I need you to stay well out the way until I get back. I'll tell the chap on the desk that poor 'Mrs Lockett' is not feeling too well, so could he please see you're not disturbed," and before I have chance to throw a rude retort to this comment he adds, "but don't worry 'darling', hubby will see you don't starve till he comes back!"

He dodged out of the door before I have chance to retaliate yet again, coming back in shortly after with a bag of supplies to keep me going most of the day, and is gone, leaving me marooned in this room with no knowledge of what's going on in the world beyond these four walls, and feeling alone, jittery, and very claustrophobic.

All I can do is sit around watching assorted tv programmes, most of which I've never even considered watching. It's amazing the amount of rubbish that seems to interest people while the rest of us are out working! It seems there's everything from early morning politics to immature couples screaming at one another on chat programmes as to who has cheated or who is the father of the baby, and folks trying to see who can find the best antiques!

At one point I find I must have dozed off sitting here on the bed (obviously engrossed in whatever programme is on at the time) when I'm woke up by a tap on the door. Without thinking, which I realise afterwards I should do, I go across and open the door just enough to peep round it.

"Hello, can I help you," I say to the smiling female face the other side of it.

"Sorry if I disturbed you, I know your husband said you were feeling under the weather, and I know from experience what morning sickness is like, so I thought I'd just check on you to see if there's anything you need dear."

I'm flabbergasted! Morning sickness, did he really have the audacity to spin that yarn to these people? Just wait till you get back Steve Lockett!

I thanked her for her concern but assured her I was just going to rest, and yes, I have got plenty to drink and snacks when I need them. Satisfied that I was alright and not about to give birth, away she went, leaving me to my 'extremely exciting' television programmes once more!

This turns out to be the longest, most boring day since I met Steve. After all, much of the time we've been together has been either exciting or scary, but certainly different from anything I ever remember from my previous life. Though, from the memories that now are flooding back to me like an incoming tide on a beach, life was always good with Jake, it certainly lacked the constant excitement and uncertainty of the weeks since that came to an end.

During this day of sitting around here waiting for Steve's return I find myself filling the time going back, right back, to that terrifying day when I'd come to in that terrible, dark, damp cave, not knowing even who I am, and certainly not where or why I was there. Looking back now on the whole experience sends a shiver right through me. I can still remember that pungent smell of dynamite from the explosion that threatened to seal me in there to die, unknown to anyone except whoever it was who did it.

I can still feel the pain on my hands and knees from the sharp rubble brought down by the explosion, and the thundering ache in my head from… what? Steve believes that someone deliberately knocked me out before blowing the cave entrance. That would certainly have been more inclined to cause the temporary memory loss, more so than the other lesser knocks I gained in my attempt to escape.

What I can't remember is the answer to the question of who did this or why even if I ever did know, but there is obviously a connection between what happened to me and Jake's murder. Steve seems to think that the idea of hiding me there could have been to make it look as if I had killed him and then disappeared, to throw the suspicion off of whoever is guilty. Either way I begin to feel as if I really don't stand much chance of getting through this. Either I'll be caught by the police and charged with murder, or I'll be found again by whoever was putting the blame on me in the first place, and heaven knows what they'll do to me this time!

As I sit mulling this over from the start I think back to that first day when I escaped my rock prison, and remember my blind wandering from the hillside to the road; I remember that awful encounter with that brute of a lorry driver, and how I made my escape and headed for civilisation in what turned out to be Chesterfield. My stay there turned out to be a genuine blessing in disguise as that's where I met Steve.

Though I have to admit looking back at it that having him take me under his wing has kept me safe for most of the time, there is and always has been, something a little scary about him, not just because of the events in Ely but somewhere, hidden deep beneath the surface, a shadow of a Steve I feel I don't really know and probably never will.

Stop it you stupid woman! I must stop my mind working on imaginary notions for no apparent reason. After all where would I be without Steve? I doubt I'd have got past Chesterfield alone. He's taught me so much about how to survive, and how to be so much stronger than I ever knew I could be, and now he had put his mind to finding the killer and clearing my name. Though he has kept a lot of his background private, and made it clear that there are things he will not share with anyone, his belief in my innocence has never wavered.

Even so, now we are so close to the place where all this happened, the place where I so well remember living an easy and relaxed life with dear Jake, I'm really beginning to feel perhaps I should never have escaped my rock tomb!

Though I'm ninety per cent certain I didn't kill him, just suppose I find it was me after all? Then what would I do and, more importantly, what would Steve do? No … of course I didn't!

By about six o'clock I'm still waiting for him to come back. Where the hell has he got to? I was so sure he wouldn't be gone for as long as this. I've picked over the odd assortment of snacks in the bag he left me but could really do with a proper meal right now. I wonder if it would be ok for me to sneak out to the nearest burger or fish and chip place? It probably wouldn't take me so long, and I could keep my hat on as a disguise. But then, I'm not exactly sure just where I'd have to go, or if I could sneak out and back without old nosey parker at the desk seeing me and offering me a lift to the nearest maternity hospital!

No, I'll give him another half hour. I'll switch the tv on again to take my mind off my rumbling stomach. Once again I'm just in time for the local news. Up until now we've only see the national bulletins, so this one seems more in depth with the goings on in this area. Yet again I find myself looking into the face of my Jake, and listening to the news reader saying that the suspected killer, Melanie Cook, is still at large following the stabbing at their home in Wimbledon on March 21st.

Did I hear that right? Stabbing? During all this time it hadn't crossed my mind to find out just how Jake died! No way could I stab him, or anyone else come to that. Did Steve know I wonder, or did he choose not to tell me? He

218

probably realised I'd be too squeamish to do anything like that, and that's why he's always said he knew I couldn't have done it.

I can't think of anyone I know who could do such a thing. Hit him over the head, poison him, even shoot him, but to stab him with what they say was a large knife; that would take someone with true evil in their hearts. I shudder all over at the thought of it.

I turn the tv off and fill the kettle to make a coffee, as much to take my mind off it as to steady my nerves. Just as it starts to boil I hear footsteps coming along the corridor toward the door, followed by a quiet tap on it. Surely that's not the woman from before checking up on me again? Perhaps I'll pretend I'm asleep and ignore her this time, but then she might panic and call an ambulance, or worse still the police!

No, I suppose I'd better answer it. Reluctantly I put down the kettle and go across to the door where, much to my great relief, I hear Steve's voice from the other side.

"Come on dear," said in a sarcastic tone of voice, "let me in please."

I open it just enough to peep round it and ask, "So, who are you this time, my brother or my husband, or perhaps you'd care to be my Grandfather for a change?" and go to close it.

"Now, now, don't be like that. I thought you'd like to have a new persona this time."

Well, I have to admit to myself (though not perhaps to him!), that it's not easy to stay mad at him for long, so I open the door and let him in. Of course his timing is impeccable, walking in just as I'm about to pour a drink, so now I pour one for him as well. For some reason, probably because I'm too squeamish to think about it, I don't mention about Jake having been stabbed. Right this minute I think I'd rather not have to picture poor Jake with a knife in his back. Perhaps I'll mention it later, perhaps he already knows.

"I'm starving," I tell him, "Can we please go out and get something to eat other than the rubbish you left me this morning? It's alright for you, I expect Andy would have made sure you didn't starve if I know him."

"You're right there. We had a real slap-up lunch at a swanky bar just round the corner from the office. Still, I suppose it's only fair to feed you too! What do you fancy, he's also given me a few quid to cover last night's taxi fare. He was too far gone at the time to remember me taking it out of his wallet at the time, so in a way he's treating you to a meal this time! Anyway, we need a fill up tonight because tomorrow we're on our travels again."

"Where to this time? Why can't we stay here for a while?"

"Two reasons. We can't afford to stay here and eat as well, and the other reason is that we don't want to stay long enough for anyone to ask awkward questions. The least anyone knows about us the better right now."

"Do you think anyone suspects us then?" I ask nervously.

"No, but they might if we stay in one place too long now."

As we sit drinking our coffee I realise I've not asked the most obvious question of him, "So, how did you get on at Jake's office…I mean Andy's now I suppose? Did you find out anything useful there?"

"I do have my suspicions but some of them are away at a conference apparently. Don't know if I really believe that though, about a 'conference' I mean. I reckon that could be a cover up for where they really are. That chap Brooks and a couple of others weren't there, so I'll need to wait to get a look at them before I can decide whether they get crossed off the list or not."

"What makes you say about it being strange they're at a conference?" I ask as this seems a strange assumption.

"Oh, I don't know. Just seems odd that they're carrying on as if nothing happened while Andy is struggling to turn up at all. Keep things going by all means, but not going out looking for more business. Not so soon, and before Jake's funeral at that. Doesn't feel right somehow. Sorry Mel, I shouldn't have put it like that."

Put like that I suppose he's right, but as he realised after he'd mentioned it, I'd not given thought till now that Jake's funeral was yet to happen. Now I realise that in the case of a murder, it would have to be put off until the police were ready for the coroner to release the body. To do that though they first need to find the guilty party.

"Ok, so where do we go from here then," I want to know.

"We'll decide on that tomorrow, but for now let's go and find food."

That being the best suggestion I've heard all day, I'm up and ready to go like a shot. As we go out the door he reminds me not to look too healthy, bearing in mind I'm supposed to be under the weather. At this point I remember that he'd told them I was actually pregnant, and decide I need to tear him off a strip in due course!

We find a convenient pub not too far from the hostel and lash out on a hot meal and a pint each. Normally I would drink wine, as far as I remember, but after the day I've had I'm glad of a longer drink. I'm so relieved to escape that room for a while, and yet in a way I find myself missing the protection of those four walls which have surrounded me all day. Eventually though, when it is time to go back, I really don't want to go but I do need to sleep.

As good as his word Steve says that I should have the bed while he's happy to lay his sleeping bag on the floor by the side of it. By the time I come out of the bathroom and go to wriggle under the covers, he is already settled in and getting himself comfortable on the floor alongside of the bed. I look down at him below me and wonder how it is that I've been happy to put my complete trust in this man who, let's face it, was a complete stranger to me not so long ago? I suppose this is that, other than the odd blip in his otherwise light hearted attitude, he's never made so much as one inappropriate advance on me. Realising this I can't help taking pity on him, so looking over the side of the bed I tell him,

"For goodness sake get off the floor. You're welcome to put your bag up here next to me, as long as you stay in it that is!"

"Are you sure you won't feel threatened," he says with a grin, "I was actually quite expecting to be banished to sleeping in the corridor let alone the bed."

"Ah yes, I knew there was something I meant to have out with you Mr Lockett! How dare you tell them I was pregnant? It's bad enough finding we're supposed to be married without going to those lengths."

"But it worked though didn't it? Kept them off your back and saved you being asked awkward questions."

I don't bother answering this, just fling a pillow at him and roll over, turning my back on him, feigning annoyance but secretly trying not to let him see the matching grin I'm struggling to keep hidden from him. I feel him move his sleeping bag onto the other side of the bed and climb into it.

Feeling the warmth from his body through the sleeping bag, or perhaps it's just the knowledge that I'm safe because he's there, I drift off quickly into a deep and peaceful night's sleep, not allowing myself to give thought to what's to come tomorrow.

As they say, 'tomorrow is another day.'

Chapter Twenty-Seven.

Here we go again, on our travels once more. We have a quick shower each, me going first this time… just to be sure I don't get cold water this time! Breakfast consists of one of those small boxes of cereal you usually find provided in these places, the sort I remember having as a kid in variety packs my mum would buy as a treat from time to time. They seemed fine back then, but now, as an adult, I could have eaten about three to make up a descent bowl full. Unfortunately there's only enough for one each, and barely enough milk to share between us! We pack the rest of our stuff into our rucksacks, along with the apples which were also there for breakfast (I'm told to keep them for later in case we get desperate!) Once again I try to find out just where we're going next, and once again I'm none the wiser from the answer I get!

Being within walking distance, depending of course on who's doing the walking, of Jake's office I'm quite naturally feeling particularly on edge as we set off. At least walking cross country as we did not so long ago, I didn't have to worry about being recognised. Here I know I'm in danger of seeing someone I recognise, someone who recognises me. To my horror I realise Steve is leading me toward the office!

"Why are we going there? I can't go in. They'll all recognise me if I do."

"Don't worry, we're not going in. I found a cosy corner where we can sit and watch who goes in and out, then you can fill me in with any info you have on any of them. For instance, you know the name of the other partner so perhaps you can point him out to me. It's him and a couple of his underlings who were away when Andy took me round."

"Yes. You mean Tony Brooks. I'd certainly recognise him, but he'd recognise me too so I don't want to be too close. I don't know who the others would have been without seeing them. I never did like that Tony chap mind you, I always felt he was looking down his nose at me as if I was not good enough."

Steve seems quite interested in my description of Tony. It seems he hadn't seen him when he went there so felt it worth watching to see if he saw him. I ask if it wouldn't be worth him calling in to see Andy again to see if Tony was back today, but he thinks that would be a bit too pushy. So we sit quietly in a convenient doorway just around the corner from the office, pull our hoods up to help cover our faces, and just wait.

To our amusement, during the time we sit here we find a handful of well-to-do business types deign to throw a few coins our way, obviously assuming (quite rightly I suppose), that we're homeless vagabonds! I'm so glad none of them recognise me as the girl who used to tread these streets on Jake Marden's arm!

"It's a shame I haven't got a guitar," Steve jokes, "I could make a killing here… even if they just paid me to go away."

"We certainly wouldn't stay hidden very long if you did that," I just had to reply, getting a sly dig in the ribs for my cheek. "Anyway, why are you so interested in Tony Brooks? Do you really think he could be the one who killed Jake?"

"First rule in investigation, suspect everyone until you've ruled them out. What do you think? You obviously don't like him, so do you think he's capable of murder?"

I had to admit that I didn't like the man but I wouldn't have thought of him as a murderer. But then I'd never thought of anyone I know as being one. While we sit here Steve quizzes me once more about everything I know about the structure of the company, and all those who worked for or knew Jake. Most of these seem pretty harmless, in fact as I tell him, I really can't think of anyone with reason to kill Jake. Even so as Steve says, with someone as well off as him there'll always be those wanting what he has and often in a position to benefit from his demise. On that assumption he says that Andy would have been top of the suspect list, but I'm relieved to know that he is no longer top of that list in Steve's eyes as he's unlikely to have the nerve. That, so he explains, is why his next suspect could well be Tony Brooks who, as the only other partner and next in line to take over the company, must be worth considering.

"Of course, you do realise that if it was this Brooks character, he'd be wanting to get Andy out of the way too?"

Hell, I'd not thought of that. I suppose Steve could be right about that, in which case Andy would certainly be in danger too.

"Should we warn him somehow, at least tell him to watch Tony Brooks until we find out who killed Jake? But then if it's not him, where next, do we have any other ideas? Do you think it could be one of those he'd kicked out or fallen out with?"

"Could be but doubtful unless they have anything to gain. But no, we can't warn Andy without risking alerting whoever is responsible, and of course, though I don't see him murdering his brother, there's nothing to say he's not in league with whoever did in return for his share of the profits."

That's something else that hasn't crossed my mind till now. I'd just assumed Andy could be ruled out. It seems that Steve hasn't completely done so!

People start arriving to this and the surrounding offices. We discreetly keep an eye on them and I fill Steve in as to who those are that I know, many being people you could say were personal friends more than just work associates. As I sit here filling Steve in to all I know about these I find my mind is in such a turmoil having to even consider that any of them could be guilty of murder.

It's not until about half an hour later that a car I recognise pulls up outside the office and three men step out. At first they have their backs to us making it difficult to be sure exactly, but I do know the car, it's Jake's! Who on earth would have the audacity to make use of his car just because he's not here? Of course, I might have guessed there'd only be one person with the lack of sensitivity, or lack of respect to use it right now, Tony Brooks! Right this minute my dislike for this man has turned to sheer hate. As for the other two men, I have no idea what their names are. I think I've seen them somewhere before but I can't remember just where right now.

Steve's voice draws me out of my reverie and back to reality, "Mel, Mel, listen to me; who is that who's just arrived? That's Tony Brooks isn't it?"

"Oh yes, sorry, I was lost in thought for a moment. Yes, that's Tony Brooks alright. A real pig of a man, don't know why Jake let him wheedle his way into the business in the first place. I wouldn't trust him as far as I could throw him, in fact I think he's evil.

As I say this I turn round and look at Steve, and am shocked at the sudden change in his expression, in fact in his whole being, not just his expression but his whole stance, his whole attitude in both body and mind, as if I'm looking at a complete stranger! What has happened to cause such a drastic change and so suddenly?

"What's wrong Steve? Is it something to do with Tony Brooks? Do you know him?

He stared across the road for a brief moment, face as black as thunder and deep in thoughts from somewhere inside his head before saying briefly,

"Oh yes, I know him alright, but his name isn't Tony Brooks!"

Chapter Twenty-Eight.

For the rest of that day I hardly dare to open my mouth. If I do it's a waste of breath anyway as I barely get more than a grunt from my companion. I wish he would open up to me, tell me what it is that's upsetting him so about Brooks, or whatever Steve thinks his name is. All I can do is to go along with him, both physically and mentally as it were, in the hope that I will be allowed in to that secretive mind of his eventually.

I gather from what he says that we now need to find our way to Jake's house tomorrow, the one that was to be our home, as apparently that is where Andy told Steve he was going tomorrow for a couple of days to tidy things up. Today he was spending the day with his parents, so Steve decided he would be safe there.

Most of today was spent just wandering about passing the time and, as far as I was concerned, trying to mingle amongst the crowd of sightseers and avoid being recognised. This time of year in the capital that was reasonably easy, though it was getting rather too nice to keep wearing my pink woolly hat. At least the last dye I'd used to change my hair to a rich auburn seemed to change my whole appearance. Luckily most of the people I knew well enough to recognise me were safely tucked away in their respective work places, a very comforting thought!

By late afternoon Steve did actually speak to me. I was beginning to think I'd upset him, but after seeing in the past just what can happen when I do, I decided it wasn't me who had done that but that it would be best to keep quiet and say nothing. Consequently I don't question him when he leads me across Tower Bridge and through the streets of Southwark till we find a convenient hostel.

"Can we afford more nights here?" I ask timidly.

"Don't worry about it. We won't be staying so very long. It'll all be over soon."

Something tells me we're obviously getting pretty close to solving the case. But where I would have expected this to be said with some semblance of pride, or at the very least satisfaction, he all but snapped it out at me in a way that I found quite unnerving. Having seen I was settled in the room, he left me there promising to return with food 'soon'. Under what name he had booked us in this time I have no idea, but as his sense of humour seems to have left him completely, I don't dare ask. I decide to take the opportunity to shower while he is out and make myself a drink. Surely, at least that can't be wrong, though I still wonder if I've done or said anything to upset him, anything that is except point out Tony Brooks.

It's fairly obvious to me that it must be something about that man that has stirred him up into a mood that seems to be like a boiling mass in his head, going round and round like lava inside a volcano, working up to boiling point... and then, when it does, what next? I feel I'm waiting for the inevitable eruption and this, with the memory of Ely still indelibly imprinted on my mind, scares the hell out of me. At least this time hopefully it's more likely it'll be directed not at me but at this man Steve says is not Tony Brooks!

I find I've obviously dozed off after my shower as I'm awakened by a loud bang! What on earth was that? I listen intently for a second feeling something drastic is about to happen, but then I hear it again, followed by loud voices and realise it is just a group of 'well-oiled' young students, probably rolling in after a night on the tiles!

A night? How can that be? I look around me, then check the clock. It says its seven o'clock but that can't be right. There's daylight creeping through the curtains and the early morning work traffic is beginning to build up outside the front of the hostel, so I guess it must be. But then why am I here on my own? Where is Steve? I realise he's always been unpredictable but this is the first time he's been gone all night without some warning, except perhaps the night he spent with Andy, but then he did leave me catered for. This time he went off without first seeing to my needs as he'd said he would!

Yes, now I think of it, the last time I saw him he promised to fetch me some food! He clearly didn't, which means I've had nothing at all to eat since quite early on yesterday, and then only a hotdog from a van we passed just after leaving our last hostel. I remember sitting eating it as we waited for the workers to arrive at Jake's office. The last thing he'd said as he left here last night was that he'd bring me something to eat, so where is it? Where is he?

I wonder if I should go out either to get food or to find Steve, but I'm well aware just how easy it would be to be spotted by either the police or someone who knows me. Certainly at this stage, it would be stupid to get caught so close to our target, at least according to Steve. No, I'll just have to stay where I am and hope he hasn't deserted me or forgotten just how long it is since I've eaten. Certainly, though I do have food on my mind, my main concern is that of just what has happened to my guide and protector, because I realise now that that's what Steve has become over the time since we met. Honestly, right now, if he failed to come back I'd be completely lost on my own.

In the corridor outside the room I've been aware of the small group of youngsters larking about rather noisily for a while now. They don't bother me as its clear they've just had a few too many to drink. I can't help thinking that I bet they'll have almighty hangovers later on, but they'll still go out again when they get the chance and the funds to do so! That's what students do after all.

Just as I'm sitting here listening to their antics and finding it quite amusing, I hear a door further down the corridor flung open so hard it bashes on the wall behind it. Heavy footsteps tell me that whoever this is is marching purposefully in the direction of my room, coming toward the group of lads who are still laughing and rolling around in high spirits, not aware of the approaching presence coming from behind them.

Their mood is immediately brought to a sudden halt by a loud voice shouting at them to "Get out of my way! Clear off before I pick you up and throw you out that window … NOW!"

Oh my God, I know that voice, its Steve, but whatever's got into him? He sounds fuming, ready to explode, and he's coming in. Hell, I can't help wondering just what's put him in this mood, and more importantly, how do I cope with him whilst he's in it? I thought he was bad at Ely but this sounds far worse. As the door flies open and he comes hurtling in like the proverbial whirlwind I wonder if I should speak or just keep quiet, so I just wait to see if he speaks first.

"Here," he says, throwing a pack of sandwiches across the bed to me, "Get them inside you, you'll be glad of them by the time today's over."

I've not long since made myself a coffee so asked if he would like one. All I got by way of an answer was a shake of the head and watched as he fished a small bottle of whisky from his pocket, opened it, and downed a good third of its contents, almost without stopping to take a breath!

I watched him doing this and desperately wanted to ask what was wrong, what had caused him to change so since he left here last night. I knew he'd not been happy about seeing Tony Brooks, but is that all this is? Is that really enough to send him out alone last night, to keep him out all night, and to send him back this morning like a raging bull and eaten up with some sort of pent up hatred. Surely not.

Whatever has caused this I have no idea how to handle it? Do I try to speak to him about it in the hope of calming him down, or will that just exacerbate the situation or worse still bring his wrath down on me as it did before when I upset him? I'm pretty sure I haven't said or done anything to deserve that again, but neither do I want to take the risk of a repeat of that day.

Timidly, holding out the pack of sandwiches, I ask, "Would you like one of these, there's plenty here?" All I get by way of a response is yet another shake of the head and to watch as he takes another long swig from the bottle in his hand. In fact he hardly seems aware of my presence at all.

Is there any way anyone could possible stop the pure rage coming from this man right now? I'm scared. I genuinely have no idea what, if anything, I can do … should I shout at him to stop and pull himself together; then perhaps risk him turning on me as he did before; or should I perhaps risk doing what my heart tells me; throw my arms round him and comfort the pained heart I feel is taking him over right now!

As it happens I'm too scared to do either, consequently I do nothing but watch him empty the bottle, then fall on the bed with it in his hand and go sound asleep, totally out of it for the best part of the day. I manage to release his grip on the bottle and throw a blanket over him figuring that whatever he has planned for our next move will not be happening for some time yet.

I'm proved right!

Chapter Twenty-Nine.

It isn't until just after four o'clock that Steve finally comes to. I reckon that bottle he came in with earlier can't have been the first he'd emptied last night, but it was the one that finally finished him off. Now, I wonder, does he have an almighty hangover, but as I can see he's still not at all communicative perhaps I'd better keep quiet. For a man who has always been full of energy and happy to have a laugh and a joke at my expense this version of Steve doesn't seem like the same man and certainly not one I feel comfortable being with right now.

I tentatively suggest a shower 'to freshen you up', but he says no, we haven't got time for that, and snaps at me to collect my stuff together, as if it's me who's been holding us up!

I dare to ask quietly, where are we going? Without any further explanation or discussion he tells me we're going to Jake's house (and mine of course, but he seems to have ignored that fact!). Speaking to me as if issuing orders he says we need to catch an underground train in the next hour or so, using the cover of rush hour to help us blend in with the crowds. It seems he's obtained oyster cards to cover the fares so that I can slip through the barriers quickly and unnoticed. When I ask what we'll be doing when we get there he just glares at me in a way that makes me feel uncomfortable and then changes the subject.

"You need to change into your old clothes you had on when I met you."

I stare at him in disbelief for a second before asking, "Why would I need to do that?"

The look I get for daring to ask that matches well the answer he hurls at me, "Because I said so!"

Needless to say, with no further question, I change immediately.

Barely daring to attempt any further conversation I have little choice but to tag along and keep quiet. Luckily, as he predicted, there a hordes of commuters heading out of London making it really simple to just blend in with them. Mind you, not so many heading towards Wimbledon are as scruffily attired as I am! It seems strange as I'm usually quite smart, but then I don't usually need to use the underground when I go to and fro with Jake … but then, I no longer do have Jake do I?

Eventually we arrive at Wimbledon station where he tells me to keep my hood pulled up to hide my face as much as possible and not to look anyone in the face. I'm more than happy to follow orders now as I'm very well aware of how close we are to what should be my home. The thought of being caught out this close would be unbearable after all.

"Where can you get food cheap round here?" Steve asks.

I point him in the direction of a particularly nice tearoom providing both hot and cold food for users of the common, and we make our way to it. I can't explain just how desperate I feel by now for a proper meal. I wonder just how much money he has left after the money he must have spent on whisky last night, but somehow he still manages a cottage pie with lovely cheesy mash on top for me, and a steak and ale pie for himself, washed down with a good hot cup of tea each.

He's still worryingly scary, barely speaking except for the barest necessities. We eat outside the tearoom to stay at a distance from the majority of its customers and then, having made use of its facilities, wander off across the common.

"Do you want me to take you to Jake's place now?" I ask him, assuming that was his plan, but he tells me we won't be going there now until tomorrow morning. "Ok, so where to next, where do we sleep this time?"

"Just you follow me, we'll be roughing it tonight. I reckon there must be plenty of places out here we can keep out of sight."

Oh no! Just when I thought our nights of sleeping rough were at an end it seems I'm wrong again! After quite a thorough look around he picks up on a reasonably cosy spot, bearing in mind it is now the end of May and nights are much less cold than the first ones I'd spent outside back in late March and early April. Even so, it's not exactly summer yet but at least it's not raining! There are no people about in this corner of the common at night and we found sufficient shelter to lay out our sleeping bags, so I suppose one more night won't kill me.

'Kill me', why did I even have to think of that expression, especially now and here! I'd not given thought to my own safety since I met up with Steve … well, not to the extent of being killed like poor Jake had been. Ok, perhaps Steve has gone a bit off the rails, but I still believe he'd not intentionally hurt me, and I'm sure he'll see I come to no harm, not after so long.

Still, I do wish he'd speak to me. I'm still getting the silent treatment, and I really don't like it. It feels as if we're strangers all of a sudden and trying to get through to him is like trying to fight my way through a brick wall with my finger nails. Perhaps he'll sleep it off and feel better by the morning.

He barely gets down into his bag before he's asleep. I suppose the combination of last night's drinking spree and that good hot meal a while ago is enough to knock him out. After all, he may have had a few hours during the day today, but he spent all the night before awake and drinking!

I can't bring myself to doze off straight away, my mind is working overtime trying to figure out just what's happened, and wondering just what is still to happen tomorrow. I lay here looking at this man sleeping alongside me, this enigma called Steve Lockett. Just who is he? Where does he come from, what makes him the man he is? And even more puzzling, why has he chosen to help me at a time when I most needed help? More to the point, why the sudden change in him and in his attitude to me just when he says we're so close to achieving our goal? All I can do is to make some attempt to get some sleep and hope things become clearer in the morning.

Chapter Thirty.

The next morning I wake to find Steve already up and packing away his sleeping bag in his rucksack. I watch him for a minute or two, and can't help but think how often I've watched him do this without realising how precisely he has always done it, not just screwed it up and shoved it in as I do with mine, but folded and rolled in that exact fashion he's always done.

I wonder if his mood has improved since last night. Dare I speak or should I wait to be spoken to? I watch him quietly for a while as he's obviously fishing things from the bottom of his rucksack and repacking them on top of his sleeping bag, presumably things he thinks he will need, but from here I can't see what they are. He has his back to me right now, but I know that whatever item it is he's just taken out and has in his hands seems to be something he's staring at, almost caressing, so it must be something meaningful to him.

Probably due to the pollen in the air, I find myself unable to hold in a sudden fit of sneezing right now, and that breaks Steve's concentration on the object in his hand. He quickly pushes it back into his bag out of sight before I get chance to see what it is.

"Here, I've got you this," handing me a coffee and a bacon roll, "Make the most of it, it's not going to be a day you'll enjoy."

I want to ask for some sort of explanation, but he's already turned away, and his attitude tells me he won't expand on what he's said even if I do ask. All I can do is make the most of the food and drink he's given me and then pack my sleeping bag up ready to go. I assume we're going to Jake's house. When I ask him he says yes, but not until just after ten o'clock. When I ask why at that time, he just says,

"He's not going to be there till then."

He, who is he I ask? Then I partly wish I'd not asked as he just says, "Your killer, that's who."

I can't help feeling a shiver run down my back at the thought that we're about to meet a man who could stab someone in cold blood and put the blame on me! Since I realised that Jake had been stabbed I've had this terrible vision in my head of him lying on the floor bleeding to death while the murderer wiped off his knife and walked away! It's the sort of thing you see in crime dramas on tv, but that's not real, this is!

And now Steve tells me we're going to meet this man. Is it that awful Brooks man, I never did like him? Or is it possible that it could have anything to do with Andy, though I know he'd most certainly be too squeamish to do it himself.

Anyway, by about nine forty-five we are heading for the house where it all happened. I still feel cut off from Steve as he's hardly spoken all morning. The house is a large Georgian building, set back from the road and surrounded by trees, shrubs and a high wall enough to shield it from the road. There are also big wooden electric gates, controlled from inside the house. Unfortunately these are closed.

It seems this is not a problem for us as it happens as Steve bunks me up on top of the wall then follows, having lobbed our two rucksacks over first. Helping me down from on top he tells me to follow him, "And for goodness sake, do whatever I say, immediately and without question!"

Any other time I would probably have laughed and said 'yes sir', but I can sense that this is no time for joking. Guided by me we approach the back of the house to make use of the assorted outbuildings as cover. Suddenly Steve puts a hand up to stop me. Peeping round into the window of an old barn type building we can see the figures of three men, two of them moving about chatting, but one appears to be tied to a central post.

At this point Steve does something I'm certainly not expecting. Having pushed me back out of sight and earshot of the men in the barn he drops his bag on the ground and, taking something out, grabs me tight and before I have time to do anything about it or make any protest, to my horror, puts tape firmly across my mouth rendering me totally unable to utter a sound! As I struggle with him in an attempt to get it off he pulls rope from his bag and before I know what's happening I find myself bound and gagged and totally defenceless!

Why? What have I done to deserve this? I'm scared and want to scream but I can't. I want to run away, but he's got me like a dog on a lead! Now he's dragging me into the barn where these others are and I don't know any of them… but hold on … yes I do. The one tied up is Andy. Why are they doing that to him? Now I come to look at the other two I'm sure they look sort of familiar, and I feel sure I recognise the voices from somewhere, but where?

"Hi boys," As they look round the shock on their faces is clear to see. "You're clearly not used to using dynamite are you? You didn't stop around long enough to see you'd done the job properly, so I've brought her back to you."

"What? Where did you get her from?" One of them blurted out. Ah yes, I remember now. That's where I've seen them, it was these two who took me to what should have been my tomb. I can remember being bundled into the boot of a car right here. I can remember now being dragged up to the cave entrance after a rough, airless journey. The last thing I think I remember was feeling a sharp bash on the head … probably the one that left the large lump and loss of memory! Now here I am trussed up like a turkey, and poor Andy not much better!

I throw him a sympathetic look, after all, I'm not in a position to do more than that right now. Between these two thugs and a wild looking Steve, I really have no idea what's going to happen, or if we'll survive the day.

"Get over there and sit down," he snaps at me, "just keep out the way and don't move."

I daren't do otherwise so I crouch down by the side of Andy, hardly daring to look at what I know is about to happen. Needless to say I'm right with my expectations. Both men come at Steve at once, and both find themselves in a heap on the floor. In turn they struggle to their feet and try again, but they've obviously not come across the likes of Steve before, even less so one like Steve in his present frame of mind. How the hell does he do this? They barely struggle to their feet before he has them back in a heap on the ground.

This must have been pretty much how he dealt with those druggies in Chesterfield, but that was fun (or so he said), this was certainly not for fun, this was vicious! He's like a madman, they don't stand a chance!

Andy looks shaken to the core at what he's witnessing. I do feel sorry for him, but then I think that right now neither of us are feeling safe amongst such violence! A few brief minutes and it was all over. Then came something which absolutely shook me rigid! He fished into his bag once more to get more rope to tie these two with, but then I saw something I'd not seen before, a large and extremely vicious looking knife!

Oh my God, Surely this couldn't have been the one that killed my Jake? Surely it wasn't Steve who did it after all, and all the time he's been bringing me back to take the blame? I really want to scream but of course I can't.

"Have you got your phone with you?" he asks Andy as he cuts him free. An extremely shaken looking Andy nods at one of the men and indicates that he has it in his pocket, and just manages to ask if he should call the police? It's clear that he now recognises Steve as his happy go lucky drinking buddy from a couple of nights back, but would never have expected him to act this way.

"No, I don't want the police involved yet. I've got work to do first. I take it 'Brooks' is indoors?" Andy nods, too shaken by what he's just seen to barely speak. "And did they tell you it was Brooks who killed your brother?" Andy nodded again.

Just then one of the men started coming to and was about to let out a shout to warn Brooks. Steve turned on him, knife in hand and, holding it to his throat said, "Either you shut up or I'll slit your throat and shut you up for good," and then, seeing the terrified look on the man's face added, "yes, you've seen one just like this before haven't you? Your boss used it on Marden didn't he?" The man nodded vigorously, keen to make it clear he wasn't responsible for that.

"We were just told to get rid of her and make it so no one found the body… shift the blame he said."

"And he told you to blow the cave I suppose? Shame he didn't tell you how to do it properly." Once again they were quick to nod in agreement.

Steve knew all he needed to know. He duly put tape over both mouths to keep them quiet, and tied them to the post they'd tied Andy to. Taking the mobile phone from Andy he told him to get out of here.

"Give me about half an hour then go to the police and tell them there's a dead soldier here by the name of Morgan who was AWOL, and who was a killer."

"Shall I take Mel with me?" he asked, but Steve said no, I was to stay for now,

"But she'll be out when I've finished what I started."

What does he mean by that? I'm still sitting here taped up, unable to speak, tied so that I can barely move and, especially after Andy's gone, at the mercy of a man I know from experience has one hell of a temper, and is right now as explosive and unpredictable as he's been since I first met him! If I could scream right now I would and I don't think I'd stop!

Without so much as a word of explanation or assurance he grabs me by the arm and marches me straight in through the French doors and into the study from where he can hear doors and drawers being opened and closed, probably by someone rifling through Jakes things.

"Well, if it's not my old pal Morgan! How did I know you'd be behind this? I think I've got something that belongs to you," as he says so pushing me forward so hard I lose my balance and end up at his feet.

It was the man I knew as Brooks, but Steve called him Morgan. Hearing Steve's voice he'd swung round with a shocked expression on his face, and was staring at me and asking,

"Where did you find her Lockett, and what are you doing here? What do you want from me?"

I could see he was trying hard to cover up how rattled he felt in Steve's presence for whatever reason. Steve was impassive in spite of the rage I could feel building up in him against this man,

"I found her where your lackeys left her, in the cave they couldn't manage to blow properly. Been dragging her round the country trying to bring her back to you. As for what I want isn't that obvious? I want a share of Marden's loot that you're in line for of course. Especially now your lads have finished off the brother like you said to do."

"They've done what? I never said to do that yet. I needed his signature on a few things first. Anyway, how do you know what they're up to?"

"Just seen them in the barn. They didn't manage to kill this one, but they seem to have had no problem with the other one out there. But then he's not much of a handful is he? I'm sure you've had him under your thumb for months haven't you? You've killed tougher than him in your time I seem to remember?"

Morgan looks well shaken, but Steve urges him on by saying, "Seems to me you need a professional on the job; you know, someone like you who can handle one of these," as he brings that awful knife from behind his back again. "You killed Marden to get his money didn't you, so if you'll give me a share I'll slit her throat here and now if you like? You know me, I've got nothing to lose so I might as well get a bit of the action like you, eh?"

I feel the cold blade of that huge, awful knife against my neck, and I think I'd have thrown up if my mouth hadn't been taped up! Whatever is he doing, and why is he doing it to me? I can feel my legs going weak.

"No, don't do that here," Morgan shouted at Steve almost panic stricken, "Use your sense man. I killed Marden here, but it would be too obvious if she died in the same place. That's why I told them to get rid of her, and to shift the blame away from me. Get rid of her away from here, then I'll cut you in on a share of it. There'll be plenty to go round after all."

"Ok, I'll dump her out in the barn with the others, your two are temporarily out of action if you know what I mean, then come back and discuss tactics. I suppose you'll be wanting me to dispose of them permanently too will you?"

"Why not? That way we can split it fifty/fifty, equal shares," Morgan says, though still with a worried look on his face which says that he's not at all sure how genuine Steve is about this, or if he's really safe in his company.

Steve then grabs me firmly (very firmly as my legs have almost given way), and carts me off back out to the barn. By this time I'm shaking from top to bottom with fear. Never in my life have I been so terrified! Then, to my amazement he turns me round, cuts through the rope which is holding me, rips off the tape from across my mouth, at the same time putting his mouth over mine (I suppose to stop me screaming, though I wish it meant more!), then he puts a finger to his lips to warn me to be quiet and hands me Andy's mobile.

"There Mel. I'm truly sorry I had to scare you to get this, but it had to sound convincing. Take this to the police. It's your proof of innocence," as he handed me Andy's mobile. He looked at me for a few seconds, as if he had so much more to say, but all he came out with was, "Have a good life, dear Mel."

For a brief moment I looked into his eyes and saw the pain and heartache behind them. I wanted to stay, to hold onto him, but he turned me round, pushed me away, and walked off back inside the house.

What else could I do? I knew I must do as he told me, yet I knew he could be in danger. After all, he was left there with a self-confessed murderer. I know he's tough, but then it seems this Morgan chap is too, and is pretty devious as well.

Chapter Thirty-One.

Steve must have pushed the switch for the electric gates as he went back in as they were now open. Thank goodness I don't have to scramble over the wall again. I really don't think my legs would have the strength to do it. I'm in such a turmoil, part of me wanting to run as far away as possible, yet part of me desperately wanting to go back to see he's ok. I don't even know where to go to. I suppose I should go to the police as he told me to let them hear Morgan's confession, but I'm worried that it will take too long when all I want to do is find someone to help Steve.

I've only gone a few yards up the road when I see what looks from a distance like black police vans, two of them, coming toward me! Of course, I'd quite forgotten that Andy had probably already called them, in spite of promising not to straight away. He was probably worried for my safety, bless him.

The first one pulls up alongside of me and a man in black with a helmet on, opens the window and asks, "Are you Miss Cook?"

"Yes, have you come to help Steve? Please be quick."

I must have looked a pretty desperate case as he pulls me up beside him for the short ride back the way I've come. When we arrive I find that there are four armed response officers in each van, all with full body armour and helmets on, and in the car behind, some sort of high ranking army officer, a captain I believe.

They pull up on the drive and get out, all except the army captain carrying pretty scary looking weapons in their hands.

"We need you to show us the best way into the house Miss Cook. Mr Marden (I take it he means Andy), tells us there are two prisoners already tied up and two men inside, is that right?

"Yes, there are two in the barn, but one of those indoors is a good man. He's been helping me find out the truth. You won't hurt him will you? His name is Steve Lockett. The one you want is Morgan, he killed my Jake."

I'd not been aware that the army captain had overheard what I was telling the police officer, but now he came straight over to me to say,

"We knew Morgan was here, he's AWOL from the army, but did I hear you mention the name Lockett, Steve Lockett?"

"Yes, I think he's gone back in there to… to … well, I don't know what to do; but Steve is a good man. He's looked after me since they tried to kill me. You won't let them hurt him, will you?"

With a sigh he tells me, "There's a lot you don't know about our Sgt Lockett young lady, but it's not him we've come to get, so hopefully we can do this without anyone getting hurt. Now come on, show us where to go."

I direct them past the barn where some of them quickly escort the two men tied there back to the van. Then I point them toward the door leading to the study where I'd last seen Steve heading back to. I can hear the voices of Steve and Morgan, both sounding loud and threatening. Morgan is saying something about how he, "wouldn't have had to if the stupid young sod had kept his nose out".

Steve, obviously at breaking point now, is saying, "What do you expect if you beat a prisoner like that. The lad couldn't take seeing it, so you knifed him to keep him quiet didn't you? Thought you could get away with it by killing the prisoner and shifting the blame on him?"

Morgan seems unperturbed by the fact that he'd deliberately killed one of his own men to save his own skin! So this is why Steve hates him so. This is why he wanted us all out of the way while he deals with him. But he won't have to now. The police will be able to take over, won't they?

I'm told to keep back out of the way but I need to know what's happening so I sneak in behind the police and am grabbed by the army captain who holds me firmly by the arm, holding me well out the way of the six guns pointed in the direction of Steve and Morgan!

Steve has Morgan in a tight grip, one arm round under his arm and round the back of his neck, forcing his head forward toward his right hand which is gripping that knife tight against his victims' throat! The sudden entry of the armed police doesn't cause him even to flinch or look up.

It's as if he's blind to anything or anyone, focusing his whole mind on his intention which appears to be to kill Morgan!

"Drop the knife and get on the floor," shouts one of the police.

"I will when I've finished the job I've started."

Still Steve stands his ground, not so much as glancing at anyone but Morgan who, it's blatantly obvious, he has no intention of releasing, even at the cost of his own life. The fact that there are six police guns pointing at him has absolutely no effect on him whatsoever.

"Drop the knife and get down on the floor," one of the police gunmen repeats in a demanding voice. "Drop it or we'll open fire."

"That's fine, he'll be dead long before your rounds hit me," comes a calm response from Steve. "Go on, shoot."

I look up at the Captain, wordlessly begging him to help, and am relieved to see that he too wants to stop this as much as I do. Signalling me to stay where I am, he steps forward in front of the police guns.

"He's not worth dying for Sergeant, come on; you've found him for us, we know what he's guilty of, so now let us take it from here."

The guns are still raised and ready to fire but, although Steve takes a second to take in what the Captain has said, he has no intention of turning Morgan over to anyone.

"For this bastard I'll happily die. You know as well as me what he did and what he's done since, and someone has to see he answers for it. Now, either shoot or get out of here and let me do what you trained me to do."

And then, seeing me standing behind the row of police, shouts at them, "For God's sake get her out of here, she doesn't need to see this!"

As one of the police take my arm to escort me out, the Captain steps forward, in a last attempt before they open fire, and I hear his loud command,

"Sgt Lockett, Drop that knife, NOW!"

Just for a brief instant I see what must be his training almost kicking in. He looked as if he may do just that … but in a split second his resolve returned. The Captain took a step back with a brief nod of his head, and the police raised their guns once more, ready to open fire.

No, no, I can't let them do this. I pull away from my escort, rush straight through their line and up to Steve, oblivious to any danger just at that moment, hold my hand out and putting the other hand on his, look him in the eye and quietly say to him,

"Steve, stop it. Give me the knife. You don't need to do this. Beth wouldn't want you to do this. You're better than this."

For a few (very long) seconds he just stared down at me. Behind that tough, killer façade I could see tears welling up inside him. I'll never know what gave me the courage, or was it plain stupidity, to do this, but whatever it was worked. He slowly released his grip on the knife, dropping it to the floor.

Perhaps because he had turned his attention to me for an instant, he must have released his grip just enough to allow Morgan to duck down and grab the knife. As he did so a shot rang out from behind me.

It was the Captain who had taken a gun from the nearest policeman and fired, stopping this killer once and for all. He's been dealt with and Steve didn't have to be responsible in the eyes of the law, but could after so long be free of this burden he'd been carrying for what must have been so long. Now at last could Steve perhaps return to being the Steve I've come to know all this time? Perhaps even the Steve I've not truly known? What would happen now I wonder? Would there ever be a chance for me to thank him for all he's done for me, to show him how close I feel to him, or must we now part company?

Chapter Thirty-Two.

It is not until now, two weeks after the incident at Jakes', that I finally get the whole story of Steve Lockett. It seems that he's served in the Paras since he joined up at the age of eighteen. He's worked his way up to sergeant, from what I hear a very well respected one at that, serving all over the world in different conflicts.

His last tour of duty was a particularly tough two year stint in Afghanistan, and it was during this time that he found out about Morgan. Morgan shared the rank of sergeant, but was not known to act according to rules and regulations. When one of Steve's youngest privates confronted Morgan when finding him beating a prisoner without mercy, Morgan had turned on him and killed him, blaming it on the prisoner who he also killed to make it look good. Steve had no proof, but as soon as they returned to the UK, Morgan had gone AWOL and not been seen since.

All this, and the long period of conflict with no leave, sent Sgt Lockett home suffering with mild PTSD which the army were planning to help with a long session of counselling and support. It seems that this may well have been accepted, and may hopefully have worked wonders but for an incident barely before his plane touched down.

On that fatal day, 18th October 2016, his sister Claire, was driving his wife Elizabeth and their two year old son,

Sean, to pick him up from where the plane was due to land at Brize Norton, when a massive articulated lorry skidded on an icy patch of road, tipped over onto their car, and killed all three outright.

Sean had been born two weeks after Steve's deployment. Poor Steve had only ever got to see his son in the mortuary and on photos!

The counselling offered by the army was tried but was never enough. It was all too raw and too soon. He had been given an honourable discharge anyway and so had thrown their help back in their face choosing to go off and 'lick his wounds' as it were, living rough, hoping to come to terms with it in his own time, thinking he could turn his back on it all and it would eventually go away!

When I met him Steve had been roaming alone for two years, thinking he must be getting better… that was until the incident in Ely. That stirred up bad memories. Even then he'd managed to pull himself together and keep it all under control until this last incident with Morgan which took him right back where he'd started.

Now he had perhaps laid his worst demons to rest. Even so, he has agreed at last to accept the help the army are still prepared to give. They've agreed to take him for a period of residential counselling and rehabilitation. The captain explains to me that this is extremely important with someone who has had that sort of training who could be extremely dangerous without proper help, but meanwhile, as it seems he's asking to see me, I am to be given special permission to visit him regularly.

On my first visit to the centre all he can do is say how sorry he is for the way he's behaved. He's clearly aware of just how badly he'd scared me back over those last two days, and in particular, the rough way he had treated me on that last day. It's taken all my doing to persuade him that I do understand now just why he did it. He had to be convincing to get Morgan to confess to Jake's murder, and he mustn't fret about it anymore. I do understand that what he did he did for me, and for the sake of getting justice for that poor young soldier who was killed by Morgan.

It takes some effort to persuade him that, with a few exceptions, and of course Jake's death, the whole thing had been quite an experience, a good one at that in many ways as it taught me so much. As we sit talking it all over I find myself reminding him of all the many more light-hearted moments on our journey, those when he took such great amusement from making a fool of me (or did I do that myself!).

Over the course of the next three months I can see a difference in him. 'My' Steve is gradually reappearing! He's going to be fine, and better still, he's talking of us making a go of it together.

Without wishing to be disloyal to Jake's memory, I know he's gone now, and I must carry on, and I like to think that, in as much as he'll let me, I might be able to help Steve accept the same about his Beth. Because I've come to terms with my loss during the time that Steve has been working on fighting his demons, perhaps we can now truly feel free to carry on working together, go forward together to give us both the support and strength we need.

I tell him that I've got enough money from Jake's will to buy a nice quiet place away from any hustle and bustle, and Andy is keen to make Steve a sleeping partner in the business, I think so that he knows he'll always have a bodyguard if he needs one! Apparently even his parents approve of this idea, thankful as they are to him for at least saving one of their sons. I assure him that he won't be expected to spend time in the city, especially as that's the last place I want to be!

He's not sure how he'll feel about being in one place all the time after living rough for so long, but I suggest we can find a place somewhere, perhaps up Derbyshire way, to use as a base then still travel around from time to time. As I tell him, we have plenty of folk to visit. For a start there's my sister Jenny and her husband who were so worried when we failed to turn up. Then we can visit Birmingham one day to see how young Josh and our friends at the pub are getting on. It was a good time when we were there, and now, even more than then, the words of our favourite song, 'Stand by me,' are so very appropriate as I know that now, 'I won't be afraid,' just as long as Steve stands by me.

Perhaps, I tell him, we can also go back to visit all our friends in Cambridge now we'd have time to enjoy the beauty of the city. It would be so good being able to be honest and tell all these people the truth about ourselves. After all, so many people had been so good to us over those weeks, and it would be great to return the favour to dear Sally in particular. I would really like to be able to help her perhaps, to afford to stay on and finish her studies, and have proper student accommodation whilst she does it.

Perhaps while we are there, I add as tactfully as possible, we could visit his family and take some flowers to the graves of Claire, Beth and baby Sean. Not being sure what reaction would come from this suggestion, I am extremely relieved to find that this seems to make him happy. Just for one brief moment he does begin to throw me an apologetic look, but I stop him before he has chance to speak and tell him there's no need … I understand now.

So it seems we'll be doing plenty of moving around in the future. After all, you can't tie down a free spirit like Steve's. I'm quite happy to do anything or go anywhere that makes him happy, even if it means going back to sleeping in old Bill's shed on that allotment. We can even chuck our sleeping bags on the floor to sleep, or grow his beard down to his knees if that's what he wants!

As for me, all I want is Steve!!

Printed in Poland
by Amazon Fulfillment
Poland Sp. z o.o., Wrocław

53035710R00157